Ralf Rothmann was born in 1953 in Schleswig and grew up in the Ruhr Valley. He has received numerous awards for his fiction and poetry, including the Friedrich Hölderlin Prize in 2013, the Hans Fallada Prize in 2008, and the Max Frisch Prize in 2006. He lives in Berlin. *To Die in Spring*, his eighth novel but the first to be published in the UK, has been a bestseller in Italy and Germany, where it has sold 60,000 copies in hardcover, and is being translated into 24 languages.

TO DIE IN SPRING

Walter Urban and Friedrich 'Fiete' Caroli are young hands on a dairy farm in northern Germany. By 1945, it seems that the war is entering its final stage. But when they are forced to 'volunteer' for the Waffen-SS, they find themselves embroiled in a desperate, bloody conflict. Walter is put to work as a driver for a supply unit, while Fiete is sent to the front. When the senseless bloodshed leads Fiete to desert, only to be captured and sentenced to death, the friends are reunited under catastrophic circumstances. In a few days the war will be over, millions of innocents will be dead, and the survivors must find a way to live with its legacy.

RALF ROTHMANN

◆

TO DIE IN SPRING

Translated by Shaun Whiteside

Complete and Unabridged

CHARNWOOD
Leicester

First published in Great Britain in 2017 by
Picador
an imprint of Pan Macmillan
London

First Charnwood Edition
published 2018
by arrangement with
Pan Macmillan
London

Originally published in 2015 as *Im Frühling sterben*
by Suhrkamp Verlag, Berlin

*A catalogue record for this book is available
from the British Library.*

ISBN 978–1–4448–3712–4

Published by
F. A. Thorpe (Publishing)
Anstey, Leicestershire

Set by Words & Graphics Ltd.
Anstey, Leicestershire
Printed and bound in Great Britain by
T. J. International Ltd., Padstow, Cornwall

This book is printed on acid-free paper

The fathers have eaten sour grapes
and the children's teeth are set on edge.

Ezekiel

Silence, deep concealment, particularly about the dead, is ultimately a vacuum that fills with truth. When I used to ask my father why his hair was so thick, he would tell me it was because of the war. They had rubbed fresh birch sap into their scalps every day, there was nothing better; it might not have helped against lice, but it smelled good. And even though a child could hardly understand the connection between birch sap and war, I didn't pursue the question; I probably wouldn't have received a more precise answer anyway, as was usually the case when my father's soldiering days came up. The answer would come only decades later, when I held photographs of soldiers' graves in my hand and saw that many, if not most of the crosses behind the front were made of young birch twigs.

My father seldom smiled, and on the rare occasions when he did, it made him look forbidding. The expression on his pale face, dominated by its strong cheekbones and green eyes, had an underlying melancholy and weariness. His backcombed dark-blond hair — close-shaved at the nape — was held in shape with Brisk, his slightly cleft chin was always smooth and the elegant sensuality of his lips seems to have unsettled a fair number of women: there were stories. His nose, slightly too short, had a barely perceptible tilt to it which added a

1

hint of youthfulness to his profile, and at relaxed moments his face revealed a roguish warmth and an empathetic intelligence. But he himself was barely aware of his beauty, and if it had ever been pointed out to him that he was handsome, he probably wouldn't have believed it anyway.

All the neighbours liked him; he was always helpful, the word 'respectable' was often used when his name came up, his appreciative mates in the mine called him the Pickaxe Man and hardly anyone ever tried to start a fight with him. He usually wore corduroy trousers, whose velvety shimmer was lost after the very first wash, and jackets from C&A; the colours were always carefully chosen, suggesting a certain refinement in the selection process, a delight in a tasteful combination, and he would never have worn trainers or unpolished shoes, towelling socks or checked shirts. Although his posture had suffered from his hard work as a dairyman and later as a miner, he was that rare thing — an elegant manual labourer. But he had no friends, and didn't try to make any either; he lived his whole life in a silence that no one wanted to share with him — not even his wife, who had coffee with all their neighbours and went dancing without him on Saturday evenings. In spite of his bent back, his continual seriousness lent him an intimidating authority and his melancholy didn't just consist of the tedium of the daily grind, didn't stem from back-breaking labour, irritation or unfulfilled dreams. People didn't clap him on the shoulder and say, 'Come on, Walter, chin up!' His was the seriousness of someone who had seen something more potent than the others, who knew more about life than he could say and who sensed that even if he had the language to express what he had seen, there would be no redemption for him.

Haunted by his past, he cycled to the mine in all weathers and, apart from his many injuries and broken bones from rockfalls, he was never ill, never got so much as a cold. But his almost thirty years as a faceworker below ground, the countless shifts and overtime operating a compressed-air hammer on the coalface (without any kind of ear protection, as was customary at the time), meant that he lost his hearing and could hardly understand anything or anyone — apart from my mother. Even today it's a mystery to me whether it was the particular frequency of her voice or the way she moved her lips that enabled him to converse with her quite normally. Everyone else had to shout and gesticulate if they wanted to say anything to him, because he didn't have a hearing aid; he didn't like wearing one as they supposedly produced interference and painful feedback. It made communication with him very taxing and made him even more isolated, even within the family.

But I, for one, always had the impression that he wasn't unhappy in this unquestioning silence, which condensed around him more and more from one year to the next. Worn down by work in the end, prematurely retired and having quickly become an alcoholic — out of shame, I think — he asked little more from life than his newspaper and the latest crime novel from the kiosk, and in 1987, just after he had turned sixty, when the doctors informed him of his imminent death, he barely showed any concern. 'No knife is coming anywhere near my body,' he'd said even at the start of the illness, and neither his smoking nor drinking diminished in the least. He ordered his favourite meal — fried potatoes with scrambled eggs and spinach — a little less often than usual, that was all, and he took to hiding his vodka from my mother in the cellar, under the coal.

When he retired, I gave him a fine notebook with a request that he use it to sketch out his life for me, record any notable episodes from the time before I was born, but it remained almost empty. He only jotted down a few words, perhaps words that were keys to his story, foreign-sounding place names, and when, after his first stroke, I asked him to describe at least those weeks in the spring of 1945 more precisely, he wearily dismissed the request and said in a sonorous voice that seemed to ring out from the hollow of his deafness, 'What's the point? Haven't I already told you? You're the writer.' Then he scratched himself under his shirt, stared out of the window and added in an undertone, 'I hope all this shit will be over soon.'

Our inaudibility to him made us mute among ourselves; my mother and I sat for days by his deathbed without saying a word. The room had been painted lime green to head height and above the bed there hung a print of a painting by Édouard Manet, *Country House in Rueil*. I'd always liked the painting, not just because of its

4

apparently weightless, almost musical execution and the summer light with which it was softly imbued even though not a scrap of sky can be seen: the ochre-coloured villa, surrounded by trees, shrubs and red flowers, with its pillared portal, also bears a passing resemblance to the manor house of the farm in northern Germany where my father did his milking apprenticeship in the early 1940s. It was there that my parents first met, and in my childhood I spent a few happy holiday weeks in the area. Relatives still lived on the nearby canal.

A manor house of the soul, on which the evening sun now fell. The plastic frame creaked in the last of the warmth, and my mother, who wasn't leaning back in her chair and whose handbag was hanging in the crook of her arm, as if she were just paying death a quick visit, set a water bottle down in the shade. Immaculate as always, having used far too much hairspray, she wore suede pumps and the midnight-blue pinstripe suit that she had made herself; when she sighed quietly I could smell a faint whiff of alcohol.

In the eighteen years that I spent living with my parents, and later, too, during my rare visits at Christmas or on birthdays, I had hardly seen a gesture of tenderness pass between the two of them, no touch or embrace, not so much as a passing kiss; instead they repeated the usual remonstrances about everyday business or shattered the furniture in a drunken frenzy. But now my mother pressed her forehead against my father's and stroked the hand of this increasingly confused man, if fleetingly, as though ashamed in front of her son, and he opened his eyes.

Still faintly rimmed by ingrown coal dust, they had been unusually big and clear for days; the sclerae shimmered like mother-of-pearl and in the dark green of his irises one could see the brown pigments. Quivering, he raised a finger and said, 'Did you hear it?'

Quite apart from his deafness, it was completely silent; not a sound came in through the window, which looked out on the blossoming gardens of the hospital, or from the corridor. Regular visiting hours were over, dinner had been served long ago and the dishes cleared shortly before. The night nurse had already done her rounds and my mother shook her head now, the movement barely noticeable, and murmured, 'Ah, now he's back in the war.'

I didn't ask how she knew. The intimacy that shone through in that knowledge was enough to tell me that it was true, and a little later he actually cried out, 'There!' and looked from one of us to the other in helpless anxiety. 'Again! Don't you hear it?' His fingers wandered in circles over his chest, snatched up his nightshirt and smoothed it flat again; he gulped, then sank back onto the pillow, turned his head towards the wall and said with his eyes closed, 'They're getting closer! If only I knew a place where we could go . . . '

★　★　★

In my parents' Bible, a shabby leather copy full of receipts from the Schätzlein supermarket, someone had underscored a line in the Old Testament — not with a pen, but probably with the nail of a finger or thumb, and although the book, set in gothic script, has lain for decades on my shelves or in boxes, the indentation in the thin paper looks as if it was scratched there yesterday. 'When thou tillest the ground, it shall not henceforth yield unto thee her strength,' it says. 'A fugitive and a vagabond shalt thou be in the earth.'

★ ★ ★

In the darkness, little could be heard of the animals but the sound of their ruminating jaws or a snort behind the feeding fence. Sometimes the beam of the paraffin lamp caught a damp muzzle with black nostrils, pink inside, or cast the shadows of horns on the whitewashed wall, where they loomed sharply for two paces before fading. The nests of the barn swallows under the hayloft were still empty, but kittens already mewed unseen in the dark.

A heavy stream of urine spattered on the cement floor, and the sickly smell of maize and bran filled the rear of the building where the pregnant cows stood in individual stalls and watched big-eyed after the man in the blue overalls, who might only have been a wandering point of light for them. They remained completely motionless, and it was only when the young dairyman had gone into the churn room that a cow, almost entirely white — it had one dark patch on its thurl — gave out a loud bellow.

Its tail whipped through the air.

'Calm yourself, I'm going,' Walter muttered and closed the door. The raw milk churns, two dozen or more, had been lined up by the wall. Dull grey on the outside, their interiors had been rinsed clean and dried, leaving a gleam in which you could see your reflection. But the cloth strainers lay on the floor between the apron and the rubber boots, and Walter snapped his fingers irritably and hung the lamp on the hook. Then he filled a metal vat with water, into which he poured a handful of baking soda and then put in the loosely woven cotton to soften. After stacking a few milking stools on the shelf and screwing shut a tin of sand soap, he opened the door to the farmyard.

A flock of thrushes scattered from the lime tree; the manor house was in darkness. Moth, Thamling's old dog, was asleep on the steps. The charred beams of the clock tower loomed into the purple sky, the gutter dangled. The shattered windows had been boarded up for now but the crest of the farm, a black horse below crossed sickles, still stood in the front garden. The portico was damaged too; the attacks from the fighter-bombers had revealed that the channelled columns, which had looked positively ecclesiastical, were hollow inside, only plasterboard, with mice living inside them.

Walter crossed the farmyard, walked through the smithy and opened the door to the calving stall. The sawdust on the floor swirled in a circle in the sudden draught. He lifted the paraffin lamp and read the notice on the blackboard

— an announcement from the office of military supplies. Then he closed the window, knocked on the water tank and glanced into the fodder racks. There was room for over two hundred animals under the huge thatched roof, but now there were just forty Black Pied cows about to come into their first heat. He whistled softly, an inviting sound, and some of them came over to the gate, let him scratch their blazes and sucked on his thumb.

Since there were hardly any pigs left on the farm, calves were now being requisitioned. A good third of the animals already bore a chalk cross on their flanks. Walter poured a bucket full of bran into the feeding trough, closed the door behind him and crossed the avenue.

Right beside the entrance to the dairy, in the old stables, lived the refugees — each family in a loose box. In the evening stillness the voices of women and children could be heard, as well as an accordion. Although the people were forbidden to cook there, smoke rose from the barred windows and there was a smell of milk soup and hot lye.

Lines full of sheets and nappies were hung beneath the porch of the dairy and a gust of wind blew something silky into Walter's face — cool stockings and a thin embroidered shirt; Elisabeth had worn the shirt last weekend, hadn't wanted to take it off for a long time, not even after the Steinhäger gin. It was only when it was 'grubby', as she put it, that she had pulled it quickly over her head with a look of revulsion and soaked it in a basin. Naked, she had seemed even more delicate to him; almost childlike, had it not been for the tuft of gleaming black hair, and now he ran his fingertips along the shirt's pattern. No sooner had he leaned forward to sniff it, however, than a voice behind the sheet said, 'Well, is it dry yet?'

Frau Isbahner was sitting on the steps to the feed kitchen, peeling potatoes by the light of a candle. She wore fingerless gloves and a tatty coat, and her grey hair was in a bun. She had narrow lips, like the two daughters who shared her home, and when she drew her chin down to her throat her goitre swelled out; a big, gleaming growth full of spider veins. 'I was just checking on the milk,' said Walter. 'Aren't you cold?'

The woman, who had a cat sleeping beside her, nodded. 'But the air is better out here,' she murmured, and cut the sprouts out of a potato. 'So you're checking on the milk. Stickler for detail, are you? What's it going to be like, this milk of yours? White or grey, maybe a bit yellow. Cool or not so cool, sour or sweet. With cream on the top or slightly clotted. Milk has been milk since Adam and Eve, you don't need to check on it.' She threw the potato into a pot and smiled at him, her false teeth slipping. 'We won't steal anything, son. We'll manage. We're refugees, not thieves.'

He smiled awkwardly. 'No one said you were, did they? But Thamling is still in Malente, so I have to do the evening rounds. Isn't Liesel there?'

'That old fox . . . ' The woman clicked her tongue. 'In Malente again, so soon? I'd like to

10

know what he gets up to when he goes out there. Still feeling his oats? Is there some young thing he's chasing after? And his wife lying sick in bed.'

Walter took out the key. 'No, it's about the tractor. They brought three men with them but only two were on the list. The third one has a form to fill in.'

She shook her head. 'Oh Lord, if it does him any good . . . How many forms have I filled in about accommodation? All hogwash. He should take care they don't hold him down there and send him to the front. Once they've cashed something in, they don't pay it back out again . . . they're scraping together all they can get. The Russkies are on the Oder, he might even be on his way to Berlin soon, haven't you heard?'

'No,' said Walter, and rubbed the back of his neck. 'I'm a dairyman, I know nothing about politics. And no one here listens to the foreign radio stations.'

Frau Isbahner closed one eye. 'Well, do you think I do? The pixies told me. The little things are quite mad after the spring. How they get about! They sit down with me and tell me about their lovely West Prussia, where the best wheat grew. If you baked bread on the first of the month and put it in an oak chest — always bread, bread on the bread board — it was still crisp and fresh at the end of the month.'

Walter put the key in the lock. Since the power station in Neumünster had been bombed, the milk, the curds and the butter were cooled as they had been a hundred years ago: water from the Old Eider was channelled by sluices through

11

the narrow brick building and the churns and tubs were set in the current. Mossy planks from the gable ends meant that the level of the gully could be regulated, and once Walter had lowered it slightly he picked up the lamp and looked into the butter churns. Cream had been skimmed off some of them, the fatless milk had a bluish glow, and he wrote his name and the time on the panel on the wall and stepped back outside.

The moon was rising behind the trees of the avenue; a big, orange disc. Frau Isbahner was no longer sitting on the step and although the kitchen door was open, he knocked on the frame. The kitchen still smelled of the pig feed that used to be boiled up here; a permanent, sour odour of turnip and potato peelings that he could even smell on Elisabeth's clothes. Mattresses and bags of straw lay along the black, mildewed walls, and her mother, who stood by the stove, was stirring a pot. 'Well,' she said without turning round. 'What does our little Walter want?'

She was smoking her short pipe with its amber stem, and he took a step into the room and straightened a picture above the dresser — a guardian angel guiding two children across a rickety bridge. 'I just wanted to know . . . I mean . . . ' he gulped. 'Could I take Liesel to the canal this evening? The people from the Reich Food Estate are donating a barrel, and there's a new band, an eight-piece. All blind or war-wounded, but they make a good racket. And I thought, because she's so fond of dancing . . . I'll bring her back safely, I promise.'

The twigs in the stove crackled and Frau Isbahner added a log. Then she scattered some salt in the pot. 'You'll have to ask her yourself, young man. She's nearly seventeen, smokes like a chimney and roams who knows where . . . I can't keep up.' She picked up the wooden spoon and tried the soup. 'You can beat her within an inch of her life and she'll still be cheeky. But if she suddenly finds herself putting on weight she'll cry, and then I'll be her 'dear Mama' again.' Frowning, she looked around. 'Tell me, what was that business behind the stall a little while ago? Why did she tip the water over your feet? It must have been hot, mustn't it?'

The grey tabby jumped onto the table, and Walter nodded and moved his toes in his boots. In spite of the ointment they still hurt. 'It was almost boiling . . . She said she didn't fancy me. Or actually she said it to her friends, Ortrud and Hedwig, over her shoulder: 'I don't fancy him.' And splat, the whole bowl! Even though I was barefoot, from treading cabbage! Luckily Thamling had bandages.'

Frau Isbahner drew on her pipe and blew smoke through her nose; she didn't want him to see her chuckling. 'Yes, women say that kind of thing when there's a full moon. It's not necessarily a bad sign. She doesn't think you're too bad, if I know my own kid. I know who her dad was, too . . . Buy her something colourful and give her a good spin on the floor, you'll be fine.'

She pushed aside the curtain on top of the dresser, scooped some cream from a jug and put it in the soup, with a quick glance at the door. 'What do you think?' she asked quietly, almost fearfully. 'What's going to happen? Are they going to take you off like they did the others? Dear me, you're just kids, you and Fiete! You don't know a thing. I let you fool around with my Elisabeth because you're handsome and you have an honest face, and then she'll end up with a cripple.'

Her eyes were moist, but Walter grinned. 'I'm nearly eighteen!' he said, standing up straight. 'But they don't need me anyway, Frau Isbahner. Even when I was in the Hitler Youth I couldn't hit a thing. Bit of a squint. And we're important here, we're indispensable. Someone's got to milk the cows and bring the calves into the world. No war without milk, Thamling always says.' He walked to the stove and looked into the pot: white beans. 'It'll be over soon anyway,' he whispered. 'The Yanks are still advancing and the Tommies are already at the Dutch border. We just need to hope they get to the village before the Russians do.'

'I see,' said Frau Isbahner, smiling again. 'Who's been listening to the enemy stations? Do be careful, son — that noose doesn't take long to tie.' She stroked the cat's back and held out the spoon to it. 'And now do a bit of work. Liesel should be at the Fährhof, I think. Kobluhn came and fetched her — that sawmill worker on the motorbike. Her and the other girls. He looks pretty smart in his uniform! If we'd had fellows like him before Danzig, we could be in West Prussia now.' She drew on her pipe, which sputtered gently, and stared at the guardian angel. 'Why is the Food Production Estate giving you beer, by the way?'

Walter shrugged and said goodbye. He walked quickly through the small park with its dark conifers. The gravel on the paths, slightly frozen in the evening frost, barely crunched, and a few deer darted away almost without a sound. Even in the back windows of the manor house the lights weren't burning; on the terrace there was a little pile of pine cones, and the kitchen door — he rattled the handle with disbelief — was locked. He lifted the lamp and looked through the pane, with its frosted decorations, at the table inside. A pepper-pot stood on it. Cursing quietly, Walter crossed the courtyard.

Since the strafe attack, the only way to get to the milkers' rooms under the roof of the byre was by ladder; the shattered remains of the outside stairs were in the slurry. There were ten rooms up there, hardly more than sheds made of boards, many without doors and only a few with windows — eyebrow dormers. Shoes covered with hay pollen stood by the beds, there were books and magazines on the chairs, on the walls were family pictures or photographs of Marika Rökk and Magda Schneider. But most of the farm workers who had lived here had died long ago. On one of the checked cushions lay a service book, on another a silver Stalingrad Cross. Walter had weighed it in his hand and found it disappointingly light.

Even though it was impossible to heat the narrow rooms, each with a bed, a chair and an

15

enamelled wash basin, they were always warm thanks to the animals beneath. Walter pulled off his overalls, turned on the tap and washed himself with the piece of lavender soap that his mother had sent him. Then he ran his fingers over his chin and cheeks, put a new blade in his razor and pared the calluses from his hands.

He put on his mustard-coloured corduroy trousers and took a fresh shirt from the cupboard on the wall. It was crumpled but white, and he left the collar open and slipped into a thick blue woollen jacket with two rows of buttons. He shaped his hair — which the barber in Sehestedt always called 'wire nails' — with some milk grease, which he also smeared his boots with, polishing them till they shone. At last he took money from the tin with the embossed Moor's head and climbed back down the ladder — that is, he slid down the struts — took his bicycle out of the empty bull's box and rode without light to the canal.

* * *

In the fields the tips of the early crop gleamed like glass under the moon, which was still low in the sky. Fighter-bombers glided past it, a little squadron heading for Kiel, you could see the pilots in the cockpits. On a marked-out meadow by the roadside, thick-coated heath sheep stood around a pile of hay and a collie darted out from under the shepherd's cart, but didn't jump over the ditch. It ran in silence beside him to the forest, its coat floating upwards with each step it

16

took, and then turned round as quietly and proudly as before. Among the high beech trees the moonlight looked hazier, and the nutshells on the path crunched beneath the bicycle's rubber tyres.

The music from the Fährhof came from a record or a radio; Walter recognized the voice of Hans Albers. The pub built close by the embankment and surrounded by darkness was lit mostly by electricity; Sybel Jahnson, landlord and ferryman, could turn his boat engine into a generator with a few flicks of the wrist. Camouflage netting was stretched in front of the bar; a canopy of pine branches over a Hanomag van and two dusty Mercedes 170s with SS runes on their number plates. Their headlights were blacked out.

Walter leaned his bicycle against the sidecar of Kobluhn's Zündapp motorbike and ran his fingers through his hair once more before he opened the door. The smoke hung thick above the counter with the old figurehead — a wind spirit in a gold dress — and the singing, laughing and clinking glasses echoed behind him across the water. Fiete's girlfriend Ortrud was pouring beer with her mother and waved to him, pointing into the hall. She looked happy, in spite of her miscarriage three weeks before, and the light sheen of perspiration made her smiling face look still more radiant. No one made their lips up as red as she did.

'It's not the end of the world,' a voice buzzed from the radio on the wall. Beside it hung the banner of the Reich Ministry of Food and

Agriculture, sword and ear of corn. Bareheaded soldiers holding cigarettes or schnapps glasses stood among the guests, chatting affably. There were senior officers of the Waffen-SS in clean field-grey and polished boots; while Walter walked towards the door of the hall he could smell the pomade in the hair of a Scharführer. His left arm was in a sling and the whole left side of his face was burned; one enormous scar. His left eye was weeping.

Helmets hung from hat stands. Elisabeth was sitting on the window seat beside the stage. In the dark green dress with the upright collar that Frau Thamling had given her, she no longer looked girlish, particularly since she was made-up and held herself very straight. Her black curls were tamed by a mother-of-pearl hairband, her mascara extended slightly beyond the corners of her eyes, and she had clearly used Ortrud's lipstick. Along with her silk dress she wore the only shoes she owned, the rubber boots in which she had escaped from Danzig, and as soon as Walter nodded to her she raised her chin and looked past him as if she were expecting someone else. But then she stuck her tongue out at him, just the tip.

★   ★   ★

Over the stage hung a banner with the words 'Fight to Victory! Sooner Dead than a Slave!'. The others had noticed him too now. Hedwig, who was sitting next to Elisabeth, stretched her arms in the air and waved with both hands.

Fiete, swaying back and forth, grinned at Walter as he rolled himself a cigarette. His hands were dirty and he was still wearing the kit in which he milked every day; steel-tipped shoes, wide canvas trousers and a moth-holed blue pullover. 'Here comes our foreman,' he slurred. 'Sieg Heil, comrade. How's it hanging?'

Hedwig — Ortrud's sister, the Thamlings' housekeeper — jammed an elbow into Fiete's ribs and Walter shook his head. 'What were you thinking?' he asked, picking a straw from Fiete's blond curls, straightening the collar of his pullover. 'Couldn't you wash yourself and comb your hair and put on some decent clothes? And how come you're so drunk already?'

Fiete crossed his legs and drew on his cigarette, which was rolled far too loosely. In the corners of his lips, as so often, there was dried spittle, and when he closed his dark-ringed eyes he looked like a girl: his face narrow, his skin hairless and his eyelashes long and curved. 'At your service, mein Führer: I haven't got anything decent to wear. Never have. And we're in the byre here, aren't we? That's what it smells like, at any rate. I see nothing but SS beef cattle.'

Now it was Walter's turn to nudge him. 'Tired of life, you idiot?' He said it between his teeth. 'Rather than mouthing off all the time, you should think about doing your work properly! What are those shitty boots and aprons doing in the milking parlour? The straining cloths weren't soaked, there were brooms all over the place and the calves were standing in a draught. As soon as the old man's gone, you let everything slide.

19

Even your room looks like a pigsty. I tell you, if he gives you another warning, things are grim. You can forget your apprentice exam.'

'Pff.' Fiete brushed the ash from the edge of a plant pot. 'Great Chief Ata has spoken. Everything must be clean as a whistle.' He took a bottle of three-star brandy out of his trouser pocket and swigged from it. 'But then you've got the bloody refugee women, Christ alive! They don't know which end of a cow is which. They'd milk broom handles. So I tell them how it works, and of course that takes time: spread on the grease gently. Don't pull on the tits, push. Finish the job, don't stop halfway, squeeze the beast dry. And afterwards don't forget to put your clothes back on . . . ' He held the bottle out to Elisabeth. 'Isn't that right, little one?'

She grimaced and tapped her forehead. 'Fiete, you're an old pig, you're so vulgar!' she said. 'No wonder they threw you out of secondary school.' Then she took a drink of brandy, shuddered and passed the bottle back to her friend.

'No,' said Hedwig, wiping the neck with the ball of her hand. 'He's a young pig. Where did you get this booze from, you crook? My kitchen?'

Fiete sank back against the window frame, puffed out smoke and fell silent, and Walter said, 'He probably swapped it for cream. Doesn't matter whether we can deliver butter, all he cares about is undermining military morale. What's a few years in a camp, after all . . . And where were *you* tonight, anyway? Weren't you going to make me something to eat?'

Hedwig, who had woven her chestnut hair into

20

braids, two interlocking hoops, opened her eyes wide. 'Excuse me? I did!' she said, insulted, and straightened her back. 'What's wrong with you today? A plate full of ham on bread, with gherkins and an egg. And even a bit of stewed fruit. It was in the room!'

She was wearing a plissé woollen skirt and her BDM blouse, with no tie, and he pointed to the key chain that dangled at her neck. 'But I couldn't get into the kitchen,' he said, and she gasped and held a hand to her mouth.

But she was smiling behind her fingers. 'Sorry, Ata! I'm really sorry. I'll make you your favourite meal tomorrow, promise! I've got another tin of spinach.'

Ernst Kobluhn, her fiancé, came out of the taproom and put a little tray of freshly poured beer down on the window seat. He too was wearing the field uniform of the Waffen-SS, with a collar patch and the black Wound Badge level with his heart. 'Long live the Reich Food Estate!' he said, and clapped Walter on the shoulder. They knew each other from the Ruhr; they had been neighbours in Essen-Borbeck. They had both planned to be miners when they left school, like almost everyone in the class, but when most of the mines were closed because of the air raids the labour office had sent them to the north. 'Well, mate, how's it going? Haven't seen you for ages. Heard anything from your old man?'

Walter took a beer. 'No, nothing new. There's been no mail since he was transferred — or at least that's what my mother says. So, what are you and your comrades doing here? Shouldn't

21

you be at the front?'

Ernst — who was really an accountant in a sawmill — had volunteered a year before, and he clapped his hand against the polished leather of his holster with a grin. 'Ah, we are, you see, Ata, we are! We've stopped doing things in stages these days. The front is everywhere!'

Walter nodded mutely and looked at the stage, where the musicians, likewise in uniform, were taking their places. Some of them had to set their sticks and crutches down on the floor in front of them before they could pick up their instruments. Fiete screwed the cap back on his brandy and turned to Ernst. 'Hello, great warrior! Another medal? Is it true what we hear? They shot one of your balls off?'

Elisabeth pinched his arm, but the other man stayed cheerful. 'Well, half and half. It was a ricochet during a punitive expedition. It's even happened to generals, Imi. Sometimes people forget to take their belts off and a bullet bounces off the buckle. But if you really must know, everything's healed perfectly, and it's all working as well as ever.' He winked at Hedwig. 'You can ask your sister-in-law.'

She opened her mouth theatrically and raised her hand as if to slap him. Fiete, who was stubbing out his cigarette butt on the windowsill, wouldn't let it lie. 'So you shoot off one of your own balls, and you call that a punitive expedition?' he asked, ignoring the expression on Walter's face. 'How about civilians, did you manage to shoot any of those?'

'What a clever fellow.' Ernst studied him

contemptuously. 'What do you think we do at the front, sit around sipping coffee? Look: the partisans killed some of our men, so we went to the villages and wiped out their families and cattle. Grenades in the stables, bang! You think I like doing stuff like that? I can still hear the screams of the horses. It's hard to bear. But that's war for you — it's not work for the weak.'

Fiete grunted and took out a handkerchief, a claggy rag. 'Grenades in the stables, wiping out families . . . ' he murmured as he pulled it apart. 'Oh, you poor sawdust soldier, what do you know? Have you ever helped a cow calve? When they get cramp because their womb is twisted? Or the pelvis is too narrow and the calf is at an angle and won't come out? It pulls your joints apart, the veins in your eyes burst. Bringing something into the world, that's the hardest work. Any idiot can destroy and kill.' He blew his nose and added in a more muted tone, 'No disrespect to you, of course. There are intelligent idiots as well.'

Ernst blanched and gritted his teeth; his cheekbones twitched. 'Fiete!' cried Hedwig, her voice shrill. She raised her sharply painted eyebrows and her anxious gaze flickered back and forth between him and her fiancé. 'You're pissed, you idiot! How can you say such things!' She quickly grabbed two beers from the tray and held them out to Ernst and Fiete; her hands were shaking. 'Now mind your manners, you hear me? I want peace in the family.'

But the apprentice milker ignored the drink and put his handkerchief away again. 'You

23

shouldn't have landed a guy like that,' he murmured, slipped from the windowsill and strolled diagonally across the hall to the toilets; the bottle of brandy bulged in his trousers.

At that moment a drum roll sounded, and the one-armed trumpeter blew a fanfare into the smoke, the signal for the dance to begin. A dog barked somewhere and the guests, mostly women and older men, embraced in the starting position and looked each other in the eye. Some of them tapped their feet or counted the beats, and as soon as the band struck up, couple after couple whirled across the floor, a dense crowd smelling of sweat and schnapps and rose water, into which Hedwig and Ernst disappeared with the rest. There was no sign of Fiete's fair hair.

'A friend, a good friend . . . ' Elisabeth, both hands resting on the windowsill, let her legs dangle and hummed along with the tune. She avoided looking at Walter. She nodded to an acquaintance and waggled her finger at her younger sister, who was pressing herself against a squaddie. 'So, what's the matter, Starekowski?' she sniggered. 'Never seen a silk dress before? Aren't you going to ask me to dance?'

She had blackened the area above her temples, where her hair was very thin, with charcoal or a burned cork. Walter was sipping from the foamless beer. 'No, I can't dance,' he said. 'I've got scalded feet, if you remember. Every step hurts. Why didn't you come by last night? You could've put some ointment on.'

But Elisabeth didn't reply, or not directly. She straightened up slightly, jutted her chin out and looked into the taproom; as she did, she pushed her lower lip above the upper, and scratched her throat with her little finger. 'Fine, as you wish,' she said at last. 'Crybabies aren't my thing. I'll find someone else.'

Air puffed audibly from her boots as she jumped down from the windowsill. She ran forwards and joined the soldiers, where Mark Hunstein, the fat local farmers' leader, immediately gave her a cigarette and poured her a glass of schnapps. He said something into her ear as he did so and Elisabeth laughed; Walter was struck once more by the fact that she wasn't really pretty. She had crooked, slightly grey teeth, her nose was far too long, she had tiny breasts and hardly any hips at all. But you still thought you could feel the smoothness of her skin under your fingers just looking at her. There was also something sparkling about her, perhaps something to do with her cheekiness, a quite special power that was less apparent in her small, always rather anxious-looking eyes than in the gleam of her black eyebrows. Sometimes he thought there was actually something of the gypsy about her.

★ ★ ★

Now the band was playing 'That Wouldn't Shake a Sailor', and the trumpeter was singing. Walter pushed his way through the dancers to the kitchen door with the porthole, and was already tugging on its handle when someone clapped him on the back. His complexion red, his lips

25

cracked, Klaas Thamling was there in a leather coat with the gold party badge on the lapel. 'Deserters will be shot!' he joked, smoothing back his sparse hair. The marks from his motorcycle goggles emphasized the bags around his eyes. 'Where are you heading off to? Is everything all right?'

Walter nodded. 'Nothing particular to report. Paraffin and salt licks are slowly running out. And the white one might be about to calve. You can see the bag of waters.'

The old man loosened his tie. 'Well, why not? Schnitzel for the final victory! And how much milk?'

'Just under six hundred litres. Most of it has been collected already, without a receipt. Did you get the tractor back?'

'No,' said the administrator, tapping his swastika and shaking his head: 'This little bauble wasn't much use.' The badge had belonged to the owner of the farm, Wehrmacht General van Cleef, who fell at the start of the war; Thamling, who wasn't even a party member, sometimes used it when he visited the authorities. 'They'd fob off the Führer, I swear. They want to give us horses instead, Polish nags, cavalry leftovers. We might as well go back to using a scythe.' He brought out his cigarette case. 'OK, I'm going to smoke a fag and have a chat with that local farmers' idiot, about milk fat quotas and what have you. Keep an eye on your mate, and don't stay up too late, you hear me? I want to see light in the stables at half-past four. They're collecting the animals for slaughter at seven.'

26

'Fine,' said Walter and opened the kitchen door. The Jahnsons had fish traps all over the place — they always had a few eels or plaice in the pan — and there was a smell of frying bacon as he stepped through the doorway. Uniformed men stood in the room, twenty or more, eating potato salad from their mess tins. Rifles and sub-machine guns leaned against the walls, some with bayonets still attached, and there was an officer sitting on a stool by the hatch.

He wore the red ribbon of the Iron Cross in his button hole, and was stirring a cup of tea. Walter gave the Hitler salute, but with his arm bent because there was so little room. Then he peered through the hatch, set a one-mark coin down on the counter and said, 'Can I get a fish sandwich, Sybel? Haven't had dinner yet.'

The music in the hall fell silent, tables and chairs scraped and the commander, whose stripe bore the word 'Frundsberg', the name of his division, looked Walter up and down. He took a sip, licked his lips and said, 'Well, if this isn't a fine specimen for the regiment. Do I know you, comrade? Have we met?'

Someone in the hall seemed to be delivering a kind of speech — there were loud cheers — and Walter shrugged. 'I don't know . . . ' he replied. 'Back in the taproom, maybe. I work here, as a milker.'

The officer pushed the peak of his black cap out of his eyes with his teaspoon. 'As a what? Why? And, meanwhile, who's fighting for the Fatherland?'

Walter took the sandwich that the landlord

pushed towards him across the counter along with his change. It was a double-decker, thickly buttered and filled with smoked eel; Walter immediately bit into it and said with his mouth full, 'I'm only seventeen. We're important for the war effort here.'

Someone nearby applauded, and the officer laughed, a mocking sound, and opened the button on his right-hand glove. He pulled the glove off his fingers with his teeth, and after he had lit a cigarette he dropped his match on the floor, where it went on burning. Walter didn't dare stamp out the little flame.

'War effort . . . ' the officer grunted. 'Hard to believe! Young and healthy, and hanging out in the milking parlour. Don't you have women to do that sort of thing around here?' He took another sip of his tea and waved Walter away with the back of his hand. 'You go back and sit in the hall, my friend, they'll tell you what's important to the war effort.'

Walter nodded, took another bite of his sandwich and went to the door without a word. The silver braid and embroidered death's heads on the soldiers' caps shimmered dully, and although hardly any of them were any bigger or stronger than Walter was, they seemed to look down on him and made way only reluctantly. He bumped into holsters and ammunition pouches, and probably trod on someone's foot; the lighting was terrible.

The musicians had set down their instruments. The guests were sitting at the tables or on the benches along the walls. Walter gulped down his last piece of eel and pulled the kitchen door shut. Elisabeth was twisting a paper flower around in her fingers and seemed, like everyone else, to be paying close attention to the speaker, that officer with a half-scarred face and his arm in a sling, and yet something had relaxed in her stern mouth, making her look gentle and very elegant as Walter tried to sit down next to her. An SS man got in his way, however; a broad-shouldered man with a dagger of honour in his belt: 'Up front, comrade. Let's have you up at the front!'

Startled at being barked at, Walter blinked into the smoke. A few streamers from New Year's Eve still hung from the antler lamp, and it was only now, as he reached for the soldier's hand and removed it from his arm, that he noticed how the audience was divided: apart from old Thamling, to whom Ortrud was pushing a beer across the counter, all the men from the area, including the oldest, the wounded squaddies on home leave, the apprentices from the neighbouring farms and the white-haired local farmers' leader, were sitting in the front third of the hall. Walter quickly wiped his sleeve and sat down next to Fiete on the bench. Fiete held out his bottle to him.

' . . . but we held our position!' the officer said on the stage and waved dismissively when someone started to clap. 'We defended our position and more: the reputation of the Waffen-SS as the firefighters of the front received its finest confirmation. 'Where we are, there is victory,' everyone knows that. And what makes

29

us so strong? Why won't we be scattered by a hail of shells?' He struck his chest with his fist. 'Because we have the right attitude, a sense of honour, and that isn't an empty word, it isn't mere sermonizing by bloodless moralists. Because when we say 'honour', men, we mean something concrete, something that benefits everyone. When we utter such a word as honour, men, we mean something quite tangible, something that helps everyone, and to which each and every one of us can lay claim.' His brown suede gloves were worn down at the fingertips, and he pointed to the circular buckle on his belt: 'Here it is, cast in metal: *My honour is loyalty*. And that means loyalty to the Führer, to the people and to the Fatherland, loyalty to the division and to our comrades, no matter what their suffering. And loyalty to our unshakeable belief in victory!'

There was silence for a moment. With his hands clasped in his lap and the back of his head resting against the panel of the wall, Fiete kept his eyes shut and made a quiet snoring noise. 'Believe me, I know what I'm talking about. I was almost killed,' the officer went on. 'Enemy gunfire had whirled around us like autumn leaves. With a piece of shrapnel in my armpit, I lay beneath a burning tank and might well have panicked. But I wasn't afraid. I knew that I could count on the loyalty of my comrades, knew that they would, if necessary, climb down into the inferno to rescue me. And so it was, men, and so it will always be: they hauled me out. We thought of the barbarian hordes, of the Bolshevik menace and our innocent children, we shook the dirt from our shoulders and charged on — on to victory!'

With his final word he stamped his heel and threw up his sound arm, whereupon the local farmers' leader and a few women in the hall replied with a loud 'Heil!' Their applause was halting, but it was spurred by louder clapping from the soldiers along the walls of the hall, and at last some of these guests even stamped their feet, while the speaker, with sweat dripping from his chin, glanced briefly at Fiete's motionless hands.

The speaker took a sip of water, and now Mark Hunstein came on stage. The steps creaked under the big man's weight. He wore his jacket open, and his belly, his waistcoat flapping over it, bulged heavily above the belt of his trousers. There was a gold party badge pinned to his collar, and when he smiled he flashed his teeth and narrowed his eyes beneath his white eyebrows until his irises could barely be seen. Shaking the wounded officer's hand, he said something into the man's burned, crablike ear before turning to face the audience.

'Thank you!' he bellowed, and loosened his tie. 'Many thanks for the great honour that you have done us by paying us a visit, my dear Frick, bearer of the Knight's Cross, and for your spectacular descriptions of events! I am sure that no one here will soon forget what they've heard tonight. Here in this room, at any rate, there is no one who fails to admire your achievements, and we can only hope that our actions and our influence here on the home front have in turn contributed something to your men's fighting capacity. Because what is it that my old friend Thamling always says: no war without milk?' Winking, he patted his belly. 'And the occasional glass of Kümmel doesn't hurt either.'

The audience laughed, someone whistled, and Hunstein raised a finger. 'I know, dear friends, you want to go on dancing. You want to enjoy yourselves and be carefree once more, and you have deserved it, you should indeed dance. Let me just say one more thing: these are difficult times, full of hardship, but as we have all just heard, others suffer greater adversity still, suffer greater hardship, and we will not hesitate to stand by them! What an abject part of the Fatherland would we be if, after these accounts of sacrifice and selflessness, we simply went on as before?'

He pointed at the soldiers along the walls. 'Who could send these brave men, these men who are willing to make such sacrifices, back into the field tonight, back into the fire, and then just go home as if this had been nothing more than an evening of dancing, free of fate and obligation? Oh no, dear friends, such things no longer exist! We too serve the Führer, we too have an honour and a loyalty that no foe can trample. Fight to the last bullet, is our motto, sooner dead than a slave, and so . . . ' He came up to the edge of the stage, which was decorated with red plissé material, and clenched his fat hands. 'And so, my friends, I will make a suggestion: that every man at this party, whatever his age — everyone who loves his family and his native soil and who can hold a rifle — should tonight volunteer to join the victorious Waffen-SS. We owe that to our heroes at the front!'

Pressing his fists against his hips, he rested his chin on his chest, and for a few heartbeats it seemed as if the silence that had fallen following his words was born of total paralysis. No eyelid twitched, no hand; just a little cigarette smoke circling about, while the farmers' leader opened wide his tiny eyes. 'Anyone who doesn't like my suggestion . . . ' he added more quietly, brushing back his hair, clicking his tongue as if he had something stuck between his teeth: 'Anyone who doesn't like it can stand up now.'

The wounded officer coldly mustered the men directly in front of the stage, and Walter gave a start when Fiete stiffened, almost imperceptibly, and gazed into the hall, in which people were beginning to whisper, murmur and shuffle their feet. A woman sobbed, briefly, darkly, as if she had clapped her hand over her mouth, and since Walter was sitting so close to his friend, since their shoulders were touching, Walter felt the quiet tremble that ran through Fiete, he heard the noises in his belly, his resolute intake of breath . . . Walter quickly reached behind Fiete's back and wrapped the fabric of his friend's pullover around his fist, stepping on his foot, his work boot, at the same time, and hissing in his ear, 'Are you crazy? Stay where you are! The kitchen is full of SS. They'll make mincemeat out of you!'

Fiete closed his eyes and sank back against the

33

panel. The wounded officer lit another cigarette, and the local farmers' leader clapped his hands once and rubbed them together. 'There we are — I knew there were no slackers here. German hearts, the Reich can be proud of you. All young men fit for military service come forward to where Ernst Kobluhn is sitting. He'll register you for tomorrow morning. Then you'll get your instructions. And now let the band strike up, if I may be so bold! Warriors need to dance too. Heil Hitler!'

Only a few people applauded or returned the salute; the musicians bent for their instruments. The one-armed trumpeter crooned 'Buy Yourself a Colourful Balloon', and Walter stood up and looked around for Elisabeth. SS men were combing the room and parting the dancing couples, unless they were both women, demanding to see the men's pay books, sick reports and leave passes, and one of them even reached for the trousers of a limping man, pulling the cuff up a little to study his wooden leg with its nailed-on shoe. And when the man's wife protested, another soldier covered her mouth with his cap.

'Idiots, all of them,' Fiete murmured, drinking the dregs of his bottle and putting an arm around his friend's neck. 'Well, bollocks to it! Come on, let's go and die.'

Somewhere some drinking glasses fell to the floor. A small group had already formed by the regulars' table with the bell in the middle. Thamling reached into his coat and nodded to Walter. 'I suppose I should have seen that one coming,' he muttered. 'As if the Reich Food

34

Estate would dream of donating a barrel of beer out of the kindness of their hearts ... How are things going to work from now on? I guess I'm supposed to make do with foreign workers or something? Tomorrow, after milking, leave all the keys on the steps, including the ones for the dairy. And don't worry about the white cow tonight, I'll take care of her. Look after your girls instead.' He ran his fingers through his tousled hair and shook their hands, something he'd never done in all the years they'd known him. 'If you get back safe and sound,' he added, 'you can always start working for me again.'

He took his leather cap out of his pocket and pushed his way outside. Cold, almost icy air blew in, and Ernst Kobluhn, now wearing a pair of round wire-frame glasses tied at the back of his head with a strap, waved an old man out of the way before frowning when Walter and Fiete stepped up to his table. 'Well, isn't this a turn-up for the books,' he said. 'Ata and Imi are coming to the front! You're going to clean up nicely. But first you're off to lovely Hamburg-Langenhorn for training, and then who knows ... You might wind up with Ivan's bayonet up your arse and get to sleep through the rest of the war in a field hospital ...

'Anyway — be out by the builder's yard tomorrow morning. Heavy footwear, light bags.'

He stamped two recruitment notices as Walter looked around the bar counter. There was an officer having a button sewn on by Ortrud's mother; another officer was reading the *Völkischer Beobachter*; while the guards beside the

35

front door were busy watching the dancers. Walter leaned forward and tapped the list, which already contained a number of names and addresses. 'Don't put us down there, Ernst, what good will it do?' he asked quietly. 'The Tommies are in Kleve, the Russians are outside Berlin — it'll soon be over. We're friends, aren't we? What's the point of making us bleed?'

But Fiete pushed him aside. 'Out of the question!' he slurred, clinging to a hat stand, setting the helmets on its hooks knocking one against the other. 'Don't listen to this cowman! He's a yellow-bellied coward. I want to fight, I'm your secret weapon, with added ricochets. Put me down as a general . . . brother-in-law!'

He leaned forward and burped in Kobluhn's face, making the latter flinch. Pearls of sweat on his nose, his lips a thin line, Fiete unscrewed his green Pelikan, the same one he had used in school, and when Walter stepped in close to talk him out of it, he shook his head and hissed, 'I'd keep my mouth shut now, Urban . . . '

Through the reflection of the lamplight in Ernst's glasses you could only just see his eyes, and quicker than the ink flowed through his pen he signed the papers and waved them on: 'Seven on the dot. Staying home is desertion. Heil Hitler!'

Walter's shoulders slumped. But Fiete saluted, muttered, 'Three litres!' and turned on his heel.

In the hall, where a dance was just finishing, there was cheering and clapping, a rhythmic request for more music, which the drummer picked up and the flautist turned into the first bars of the 'Königgrätzer March'. Ortrud manoeuvred her way through the guests with a tray full of broken glass. Her flaxen hair was loose and tears ran down her cheeks, and when she untied her apron strings her hands were trembling. Yet she was trying to smile: kissed and hugged her boyfriend, whispered something in his ear, then she looked at Walter and said, 'You'll watch out for him, won't you? He's such a stupid boy.'

'I'll try,' Walter replied. 'Don't worry. It'll probably all be over before we've finished training.'

Ortrud's mother passed a drink across the counter to him, a pale golden aquavit in a glass covered with condensation. Now the band was playing 'A Night Full of Bliss', and he craned his neck to look over the dancers. Elisabeth was smaller than most of the guests, and as he couldn't see her mane of hair with its mother-of-pearl hairband, he bent down a little and searched among their legs for her boots, also in vain.

Hedwig was dancing with the farmers' leader and waving; Walter held out the palms of his hands and mouthed her friend's name. She shook her head, so he waved too and left the pub.

It was colder now; lone snowflakes fell almost vertically over the canal. Cigarettes glowed in the cabin of the Hanomag van, and beneath the tarpaulin there were men laughing and a woman squealing. The handles and leather saddle of Walter's bicycle, wrapped in raffia, were ice cold, and he rode slowly through the little forest of

37

beech trees where the frozen puddles crunched under his tyres. The stalks of winter wheat along the road, previously stiff and transparent in the moonlight, now hung down in all directions beneath a coat of frost.

The shepherd's hut and the moorland sheep were no longer to be seen, and no light burned in the semi-circular windows of the feed kitchen. There was hardly any washing on the lines as Walter rode to the farmyard, opened the stable door a crack and pushed his bicycle into the bull's box. Then he lit the paraffin lamp and climbed the ladder to the milkers' rooms. Frost also glittered on the moss between the bricks. The unpainted floorboards — you could look down at the hayloft and the byre through the chinks — bowed under his footsteps.

The curtain, a threadbare sheet of jute, was not fully drawn. Moonlight shone into the room, and the first thing Walter saw was the dress hanging neatly over the back of the chair, a paper flower in its button hole. Rubber boots stood at the end of the narrow bed, and when he slowly lifted the lamp — its light was faint, its flame flickering — Elisabeth put her hand over her eyes. She had put on fresh lipstick, and the visible pulse in the vein in her throat and the deep black of her armpit hair took Walter's breath away for a moment. With a hand pressed against the slope of the roof, the dry thatch, he trod on his heels to get his boots off. The iron bed creaked. 'I hope you're going to turn that light out soon!' Elisabeth whispered and edged sideways. 'Otherwise I'm off.'

Only the gate of the actual barracks was still undamaged, a massive brick arch. The roof of the commander's office had been blown away, rain rattled on the tables, drenched carpets sagged under the plaster. But in the hut on the edge of the clay pit it was warm. That afternoon the Stabsscharführer had ordered them to stay indoors, and almost all the recruits — twenty-four of them shared the room — lay on their beds writing letters, playing chess or just dozing. Damp socks and forage caps steamed on the flue, and the wood in the stove gave off a resinous smell.

Their quarters were covered with tarpaulins which in turn were covered with brushwood, camouflage which had also been employed on the transporters and anti-aircraft guns hidden among the trees, and although the British had stopped bombing army barracks some time ago — because, it was secretly suspected, they soon planned to move in themselves — a few heads always rose whenever the wind made the tarpaulins clatter. The noise was very much like that of the fighter-bombers that flew over the area more and more frequently, sometimes even during the day, and shot at everything, even cattle. Visible a long way off in the flat landscape, stable roofs could be seen smoking: the smouldering thatch.

Walter went to the window and opened the package that his mother had sent him. Raindrops and the occasional hailstone tapped

39

against the pane. The seven women from the nearby camp, who worked in the unit, stood huddled under the rusty sheet of corrugated iron that served as the porch of their weather-beaten shed. Needle-thin trickles ran through the holes in their makeshift shelter onto their shorn heads and into the necks of their overalls and jackets. They were all looking down. Their guard, in his long cape, pulled his dog off the platform when a wagon trundled down the slope. Its brakes squealed.

The parcel contained cigarettes, a tin of cola chocolate, some fruit loaf with candied lemon peel and a photograph of the ruins of their house. Walter threw Fiete, who was sitting on a stool dabbing at the blisters on his feet, a pack of Overstolz cigarettes. Little Sven Jacobsen from Elms-horn, who had been in the bunk above Walter's for two days, whistled through his teeth. 'You seem to be doing all right!' he whispered. 'I'd like a mother like that.'

The house in Essen was only a pile of bricks now; a piece of chimney and the stairs protruded from it and Leni's harmonium lay in the garden, or rather the charred remains of it did. 'My mother's doing all right, anyhow,' Walter said, and shoved the tin of chocolate under his pillow. 'She has a new crush, an undertaker, and I keep getting cigarettes.' He handed Sven a pack as well, and sat down at the table with his letter. 'The only problem is that I don't smoke.'

His mother had used a blue pen. She must have licked the tip from time to time; the first

40

letters of certain words were a slightly deeper colour:

I'm glad you're still in the barracks. Maybe the final victory will come soon and you won't ever have to leave! Everything's in a state of chaos here. Thank heavens we were in the bunker when the bomb fell. Herbert is good to us, we help him in the shop. He always has a lot of coffin makers around, because people are always dying, as they put it so nicely, but at the moment, sadly, he's got even more than usual. His house, the gatehouse at the old cemetery, you know it, hasn't been touched so far. There's a door in the basement leading even further down, into the catacombs. It used to be cisterns — the water store for the brewery! — and now they have bones stacked in it, gruesome. But there's no better place in an air raid, you hardly feel a quiver.

I haven't heard a thing from your father — luckily, I almost said. That thing about demotion is probably true. Old Krüger, who also works in Dachau and is on holiday here because of the direct hit, confirmed the story for me. Apparently, your father gave some cigarettes to those criminals or whoever is locked up in there, half a pack of Ecksteins. One of the other guards spilled some beer during a card game, and the butts were put on the stove to dry. They almost fried to a crisp and so no one wanted to smoke them. Your father gave them to the inmates, and for that they shipped him who knows where.

The light changed, and Walter looked up; a

41

truck with a wood carburettor was pulling up outside the hut.

And many Happy Returns! If you need anything let me know. We are doing reasonably well, Herbert sets his own prices. No one can tell me how many marks I need to handle a corpse, he always says, and it's true! Sometimes I smell something on his hands, but maybe it's my imagination, because he's very clean. And now I will stop. (Good heavens, eighteen . . . Do you have a photograph of yourself, in uniform?) Warmest greetings from your M.

Walter turned the damp socks and caps over on the flue and pushed the letter into the embers. A draught whistled through the cracks in the window and, even though it was still pouring rain, the women came out from under the porch and began unloading sacks from the truck. Where the sacks were open, papers, rusty tins and ragged prison uniforms spilled out, which they gathered up before dragging everything to the water-filled clay pit, which didn't seem to be very deep. The contents sank just below the muddy surface, and for a moment it looked as if the guard's dog, a Rottweiler, was running over the top of the water.

The door was pushed open, a stool fell over. The recruits, almost all in black training uniforms with runes on their chests, jumped from their beds and stood at attention. Some groaned, and Untersturmführer Dr Rapp, 'the snapper', as they called him, briefly raised his arm in salute before examining the feet of his men, sore from the forced march. Grinning, he turned on the ceiling light.

He had a medical bag with him, and put a razor, a packet of cotton wool and a handful of small metal ink-stamps peppered with needles on the table. Then he uncorked a chemist's bottle, poured a clear liquid into two kidney-shaped bowls and unscrewed a bottle of ink. 'So, listen here,' he said, lowering himself onto the chair. 'You're going to get a tattoo of your blood group. A soldier should always have it in his head, but who knows where your heads are right now . . . A little joke. Show me the inside of your left upper arm and get ready for a tiny little prick.'

He took off his cap, looked at a piece of paper and nodded to the pockmarked Jörn Asmussen, the senior soldier in the quarters. After disinfecting the spot with cotton wool, the doctor dipped the appropriate stamp in some ink, pulled the skin taut with thumb and forefinger and stuck in the needles to the hilt. Then he handed the man a plaster and crossed his name off a list. 'Incidentally, you may have to get rid of that mark, some day,' he said. 'History is capricious. In that case I advise you to stub out a cigarette on it. Sturmanwärter Caroli, A-positive, step forward!'

Fiete rolled up his sleeve and hobbled to the table; the officer looked up at him, shaking his head. 'Well look at this, if it isn't our aesthete. Dance shoes too tight again last night? Iodine may help, son, but it'll heal faster if you piss on your feet.' A few recruits sniggered as the doctor took some cotton wool from the packet and used it to wipe the face of his watch: 'I'm not joking, men, it's true. Urine is sterile if you're healthy. Pee on your wounds, even in the field, and everything will heal three times as fast.'

He pressed the stamp into Fiete's skin, and the boy closed his eyes tight and groaned through gritted teeth, 'I wish to report, Untersturmführer, that I've also got blisters on my heels.'

The officer, lips pursed, studied the bloody tips of his needles and nodded. 'Yes, that's tough, I quite understand ... And of course it takes a manhood of remarkable dimensions and a bit of flexibility not to spill it all over yourself.' He winked at the assembled company. 'You'll just have to get someone else to piss on your feet, won't you?'

Some pulled faces, others laughed, and even Fiete grinned. He rested his hands on the table, almost touching the officer's cap, accepted the plaster and asked amid the general hilarity, 'Are we actually still going to be deployed, Dr Rapp?'

Immediately they all fell silent, and their superior threw the stamp into one of the bowls. Then he leaned back in his chair, clasped his fingers over his belt buckle and looked at Fiete's hands until he drew them back. 'Still?' the doctor asked, frowning. 'What do you mean *still*, Candidate Caroli? How am I supposed to understand that word?' He smiled vaguely, almost wistfully; spruce logs crackled in the stove. 'Should I understand it at all?'

He dismissed Fiete with a nod, and after all

the men had been tattooed he walked to the sink in the corner, washed out the stamps and bowls and put them back in his bag. Finally, he snapped his fingers: 'So, candidates, listen up!' He waited until everyone was at attention, and looked past the recruits to the pit outside. His lids hung wearily over his pupils. 'Of course you will not be deployed,' he said in an almost paternal tone, and there were sighs of relief from the men. Fiete winked at Walter.

'That's about the stupidest question you could've asked! You already *are* being deployed,' he went on. 'This is the end of basic training, even though you've spent only three weeks in barracks instead of the usual three months — you can now call yourselves members of the Waffen-SS. Your company, with all of its Scharführers, will join the troops outside Budapest; at nine p.m. the transporters will be in the yard. Beds are to be stripped, cupboards cleared. I don't want to see a toothpick left here! Sieg Heil!'

He reached for his bag and turned to leave. When the door had closed behind him, many of the young men dropped onto their beds and cursed quietly. Fiete swept a few chess pieces from the board with the back of his hand, then lit a cigarette and joined Walter at the window. Walter was eating a piece of the fruit loaf, letting it slowly dissolve on his tongue.

The rain rattled against the glass, which was cracked — a silver line. All the sacks were now in the pit. In the huts over by the pit — you could only see the rooftops, a few chimneys, no smoke

— a bugle sounded for evening roll call, and the women, whose clothes stuck to their backs, slowly pushed the wagon back up the steep slope. The dog snuffled at their legs.

The puddles outside quivered in a breeze, the long roots of bushes and trees dangling from the various exposed layers of earth swayed, and Walter wiped condensation from the pane of glass, closing his eyes tightly. For a heartbeat he could still believe that he hadn't seen what he thought he'd seen through the mottled glass, and he nudged Fiete in disbelief. But something was definitely moving in the pond, there was twitching under the mud-coloured jute; a knee could be discerned, perhaps an elbow, the suggestion of a thin face. And a moment later it was under the water.

★   ★   ★

Dear Elisabeth, we have to leave here after all, so I'm writing to you quickly, because this is my last chance. My time here has been torture, but at least I've got my driving licence, for all classes of vehicle, which is also valid in civilian life. So you can start choosing what I will soon be driving you about in. Maybe an armoured car? I received your card, you're very lazy. Even my sister sends me more mail and she has tuberculosis. What do you mean by 'One, two, three'? I can just about imagine, but it would be nicer if you could write it out in a letter. I hear from old Thamling that you have to do the cows now, and that serves you right. You'll be able to see how hard we work. Fiete sends his best, of course

46

he had a dirty joke at the ready, something about milking stools and so on. Now we're packing our stuff, we're off to Hungary, and once we have a field post number I'll send it to you so that you can write to me. Or you can go to the central issuing agency in Erfurt and write 'at the front' underneath my name, and that will get there too. Unless I'm 'under the ground' by then. But I don't believe I will be, because I have this one clear memory that protects me. One, two, three.

★ ★ ★

During the night they had reached the outskirts of Ingolstadt, where the forty men in the platoon were to be quartered in a workshop warehouse; a barn on the edge of a forest. It had been freezing on the back of the transporter, so everyone was crowding round the stove and getting snapped at because they were in the way. The previous evening a medical unit had set off too early and found themselves in the sights of American fighter-bombers: the survivors, some of them in bandages, were working with the men from the maintenance troop to repair their van — a badly riddled Opel Blitz with a box body — so sleep was out of the question amid all the sawing, hammering and soldering.

The troops sat around on bales of straw and smoked, and when volunteers were needed to fetch food from the village, almost all of them put their hands up. The two lidded enamel buckets needed two soldiers each to carry them, on shoulder poles, and Egon Vatteroth, their

Scharführer, pushed his cap off his forehead and scoured the thinly clouded sky before waving them through the gate towards the country road. 'Keep your eyes open!' he called after them. 'I don't want to be left with a hotpot of human flesh. The Yanks have impeccable targeting devices — they'll shoot the cigs out of your mouths.'

He had selected Ole and Harry Laatz, twins from near Plön, as well as Walter and skinny Paul Jeppsen, and the men walked quickly down the path; a lane through yellow grass that wetted their coats. They stuck closely to the pollarded willows by the ditch, their broom-like buds already blossoming here and there, and Paul, a farmer's son from somewhere near Husum, pulled off a twig and said, 'Someone should cut off these witches' brooms, or they'll turn into weeping willows.'

'Nonsense,' said Ole, who shared a shoulder pole with Walter. 'Leave something for the bees. No need to do anything before the catkins are out.' The twins, who barely resembled one another, came from the country; freckled Ole had been doing an engineering apprenticeship in Flensburg when he'd been collected from the courtyard of the technical college three weeks earlier and brought straight to the barracks. 'Our father often trimmed them in the winter, because there was nothing else to do. And then we had to weave them into those bloody fences, like women. Wasn't that a pain, Harry?'

'Nah, not really,' said his brother. 'I liked doing it. 'Specially if Hilde was there.' He looked

48

at Walter. A bit plumper than his brother, he had been attending the agricultural college in Kiel; soldiers from the Frundsberg Division had surrounded the Gloria Cinema and declared all the men who came out to be volunteers. 'Our cousin, Hildchen, remember? You've never seen anything so filthy. She pulled the bark from the slippery willow branches like it was a condom and . . . ' He groaned. 'I can't put it into words. I went to see that film with her, *Romance in a Major Key* or whatever it was called, back row. And guess where my hands were?'

'Shut up!' hissed Paul, and they all stopped and stared into the clouds, which were scattered against the pale blue March sky — but he just squeezed out a fart, a high note like the sound of a toy trumpet, and they walked on laughing. The path turned into a paved road leading downhill between hop fields, and the sound of their heels grew louder as they passed through a railway embankment. In the dip behind the tunnel was the village, four or five farmhouses, a pub and a brightly painted church. The wall below the onion-shaped dome was supported by struts, and you could see into the belfry to the empty headstock. A hawk crouched between the rafters.

Two Wehrmacht motorbikes stood outside the pub, uncamouflaged. The heavy door creaked on its hinges and as the boys stepped into a corridor full of cupboards and dressers they were surrounded by a cool silence, filled with the smell of yeast and cooking fruit. The black stone slabs on the floor shimmered in the candlelight that flickered in front of a crucifix, a poster on the wall showed the crooked shadow of a man with a hat and a turned-up collar. Ole called out, 'Heil Hitler, my friends! Is anyone there? We're the soup troop.'

Pigs squealed somewhere. At the end of the passageway a door was pushed open and a young woman in a sleeveless apron came out of the stable. 'Damn. You lot here already?' Her hair was tied up at the back of her neck and for a moment it looked as if she was wearing red gloves. There was fresh blood on her rubber boots as well, and when she noticed the boys staring at her bare knees she couldn't help chuckling. 'We're slaughtering,' she said, and pointed with her knife to the kitchen, where a stone pot sat on the fire. 'Help yourselves. There are bags of bread in the bedroom.'

The stable door closed. Splashes of grease on the kitchen wall ran in the patch of sunlight that fell through a barred window and trickled away into the shade. 'Well, heavens above,' said Ole, bending over the pot. 'What sort of soup is this supposed to be? Looks like tomorrow's shit, doesn't it?'

The over-boiled lentil stew, with black onions floating on the surface, smelled like vinegar, and while occasional slices of potato were apparent, not a single piece of meat could be found. 'No,' his brother replied and licked his finger. 'Yesterday's.'

Paul took a few ladles from the pile of cutlery in the sink, and while his comrades scooped the tepid brew into their buckets, Walter opened the hatch and peered into the pub. It was gloomy in there too, in spite of the bright noon hour; in the thick walls the windows looked like arrow slits. A fair-haired boy in knee breeches, sitting on a stool and reading, replied to Paul's 'Heil!' with a timid 'Grüss Gott!' He let his feet dangle in his alpine shoes and glanced once towards the stove in the corner, a warning nod.

Walter leaned forwards and before he could make out the faces of the two men sitting there at a table in a pall of cigarette smoke, he saw the gleam of the gorgets on their chests, like polished silver. Empty beer mugs stood in front of them, as well as plates with the remains of food and a basket containing an untouched white loaf. They wore field uniforms, buttoned to the throat, and according to their collar patches they held the rank of Hauptscharführer. One of them was greying at the temples, and the other, thinner, who was missing three fingers on his right hand, drew on the stub of his cigarette and said, 'So, what are you staring at, like a great cow? Can't you say hello? Out you come, all of you!'

Walter shut the hatch, buttoned up his coat and hissed, 'Guard dogs!' Paul spat on the floor. They all straightened their waist belts and forage caps. When they stepped into the public room through the swing door, the boy had disappeared; his book, The Last of the Mohicans, lay on a barrel. The recruits saluted dutifully and stood to attention, waiting. By now the secret military policemen had put on their caps with aluminium braid; the thin one wore white gloves, the missing fingers stuffed with fabric. Two

51

sub-machine guns leaned against the bench at the head of their table below a painting of the Madonna with flaming heart.

Flies buzzed in the embrasure of the window, and the greying man took a pair of glasses from his pocket, pointed them at Harry and said, 'Pay book and travel orders.' There was a matchbox beside his plate, and Walter could see that it was printed with the same motif as the poster they'd passed in the corridor; beneath the broad shadow of a man it said, in bright yellow writing, 'Pst! The enemy is listening!'

Harry took out his neck pouch, stepped up to the table and said, 'Reporting for duty, sir. We're out collecting food.'

The officer frowned. There was a dark green wooden box, scratched at the edges, on the bench beside him. He nodded Harry back into rank and opened his pay book, which contained no entries yet, apart from his personal details. In the photograph Harry had pomade in his hair and was wearing a civilian suit and tie. A gold-coloured Storck sweet wrapper slipped from between the book's pages. 'Does that mean you have no travel orders?'

'We're only food collectors,' Paul chimed in; the officer jutted out his chin and brought the flat of his hand down on the table.

'Do you think I'm deaf or something, private? You'll speak when I tell you to speak — has no one taught you that?' He studied the boys through narrowed eyes. Beside the two officers' beer mugs were smaller glasses painted with gentian flowers, also empty. The grey-templed

52

officer ran his thumbnail through the gaps in his teeth and pointed at Ole with the little finger of the same hand. 'Which company?'

Ole swallowed hard and said hoarsely, 'Respectfully, sir, we haven't been assigned yet. We've come from the shortened basic training in Hamburg-Langenhorn, forty recruits, Scharführer Vatteroth.'

'Weapons? Vehicles?'

'K98 carbine, stick grenades and handguns. Two Vomag transporters.'

'Quarters and march direction?'

Walter, standing next to Ole, turned his foot on his heel, nudging him, but Ole reached out and pointed vaguely: 'A kilometre north of here, in the Waffen-SS workshop warehouse. When it's dark we're moving on to Graz, or more precisely to Adelsried, where we'll be assigned to different divisions. We're really only collecting the food for our platoon.'

The officer with the stuffed glove, who had been taking notes, put his notebook away and opened a silver case that held oval cigarettes. 'And we're supposed to believe that, are we? How stupid do we look?' He tapped one of his cigarettes firmly on the case. 'You're all well behind the front lines, where there shouldn't be a troop transport anywhere around. You aren't wearing helmets or insignias, and you have no passes or marching orders. We don't even have a sick note, and it isn't at all clear to me how you could have ended up in this dump, given your supposed direction of travel.' The flame of a match reflected in the metal half-moon that

53

hung at his chest. 'Have you come to visit Grandma?'

The recruits all grinned — no one answered — and the greying man looked at his watch, a black chronometer for pilots, and put on his gloves. 'Right, then, comrades,' he said, 'we're going to check your statements. They'd better be correct: no one can hide from us, not even at their grandmother's house. If not, you'll find yourself hanging from the nearest tree quicker than you can say 'desertion'. Now get out of my sight!'

The boys clicked their heels, saluted and went back into the kitchen, where they scooped what was left of the soup out of the pot and into their buckets and tied the bags of bread to their belts. Their burden was heavy; Walter used his cap as a grip, the others did the same, and they left the pub in silence and crossed the street to walk in the shelter of the stable walls. There wasn't a cloud in the sky now, and in front of the church the first crocuses gleamed in the sun, white and purple.

'Christ, they were a pair,' said Ole, after they'd left the village behind. 'Sticklers for the rules. I'd like to meet them in civilian life, over a barrel of beer. Why did you kick me?'

Paul and Harry were already in the tunnel; startled bats fluttered out from under the arch and Walter looked around. 'Well, because telling the truth didn't seem like such a great idea,' he said in a hushed voice. 'Those guys wore SS uniforms but they were riding Wehrmacht motorbikes. And they had a radio telephone

54

and foreign cigarettes.'

The rope loops creaked and their bucket banged against Walter's calves when Ole came to an abrupt standstill. 'Why? What's that supposed to mean? Do you think they were working for the other side or something? Bastards like that, here in Bavaria?' He rubbed his nose. 'Oh, nonsense. No spy would dare come so far behind the lines. All that gear might just have been looted from prisoners or downed pilots.'

Walter shook his head. 'My workmate, a master milker who snuffed it last year, was in the military police as a volunteer. He even had the Iron Cross. Those guys know exactly which soldiers are passing through their territory, or else they wouldn't be military police. Weaponry, troop strength, vehicles, where they sleep and where they're headed — guys like that don't need to ask questions. They'd have had it all radioed in before we even set off.'

Ole opened his mouth but didn't say anything. The rattle of engines came from somewhere behind the houses and barns, and he and Walter both looked back towards the village. The hawk was still sitting in the belfry, cleaning its feathers, but the square in front of the pub was empty apart from the woman in the apron. She was fondling the coat of a little dog and letting it lick her hands; Walter and Ole stepped out of the underpass into the narrow road striped by the shadows of the hop poles and hurried to catch up with the others.

Harry, with a cigarette between his lips, sparked his lighter. 'I'd marry her,' he said over his shoulder to Paul. 'I would. We're not first cousins, you know. So there'd be no wonky kids. We like chatting too, and she wrote to me at the barracks about getting married. But now I'm working for Himmler . . . The wife of an SS man is supposed to be at least five foot three, he said. My little one would have to stretch a bit, she's only five one and a half.' He reached behind him and gave Paul the cigarette. 'Well then, I'll just marry a tall woman and we'll lead a double life, like in that film *Romance in a Minor Key*. Have you seen it?'

Paul said he hadn't and took a deep drag. Cobwebs floated through the air, which stank of brackish ditch water, and it was probably because of the direction of the wind that they didn't hear the aeroplane sooner. It was a single-engine fighter-bomber, silvery grey, and soup slopped out from under the lids as they set their buckets down and dropped the poles to press themselves against the willows. They could see the numbers on the plane's fuselage, could see a white star in a black circle, and the pilot up in his glazed cockpit — who had, of course, spotted them long ago — raising a hand.

He actually seemed to be waving, so that for a wink of an eye they could almost believe that the bombs released a little ways from them were meant for quite a different target. But they didn't fall vertically, of course. They spun shimmering in the spring breeze and almost collided before, a fraction of a second after the boys had thrown themselves into a ditch, they detonated on either side of the road, deafening them. All Walter saw of the explosion before mud splashed over his face, his cheek in the rotten grass, was Paul's open mouth distorted in a scream. Soil spraying up from the field darkened the sky and the hop poles whirled into the air before plummeting back to the road like a rain of spears, silently.

The loaves slipped against the back of his neck. Something brushed his leg. A piece of shrapnel lay smoking on the edge of the ditch, dark purple, and when he straightened up again the shaft of his right boot flipped open. But apart from a scratch his calf was uninjured, and the others had clearly been lucky as well. The buckets lay in the field, crushed like tin cans. The recruits stood back up, knocking lentils and dirt off their coats with their caps among the heads of the willows, which the shock had torn from their trunks. Everyone was as pale as a ghost; they were breathing with their mouths open, and Walter, still halfway in the ditch, retrieved a loaf and tried to wipe it clean with his sleeve. It was yellow with catkin dust.

★　★　★

Most of the boys, wrapped in blankets and tarpaulins, were still asleep when the transports drove into the tunnels near Adelsried at dawn. Aside from the natural caves, running with spring water, these consisted of wide tunnels dug deep into the mountain, supported with steel and concrete pillars and lit by electric light. Barking echoed inside; horses and donkeys, some saddled or loaded with luggage, dozed along the greyish-white limestone walls where canisters and boxes of ammunition, rolled-up tank tracks and bags and cases full of food were stacked. Signs hung under the arches, and among the trucks and cars parked on marked areas rough wooden steps led to lofts full of bunk beds.

Even though it was early, there was a great deal of work going on. The pecking sound of chisels or pickaxes sounded from the caves, and the clatter of typewriters from behind hardboard partitions. Mechanics were repairing an officer's car with light-blue standards and blood-smeared windows; doctors and nurses were treating the wounded, who lay on straw in a passage off to the side; and Russian prisoners in dusty uniforms carried baskets full of rock out of the tunnels and emptied them on the slope beside the entrance, where a guard was rolling a cigarette.

From here one could look out over the forested valleys to Graz, a few steeples in the rosy morning haze, and after the new arrivals had washed by a trough — turpentine soap hung above it on wires — Scharführer Vatteroth led them into a dining hall; a big cave lit by two or three bulbs.

Even though countless soldiers and a few civilians were sitting at the long tables, there was little noise in the room save the scratch of knives and spoons on tin plates and the occasional murmur. Some people were cooking in the cave too, but the prevailing smell was not so much grease and acorn coffee as sweat, pus and urine.

Hardly anyone wasn't wearing a bandage, and there were few bandages that didn't need changing. Sticks and crutches leaned against the glimmering rock walls.

As they began to eat, the boys looked furtively at the unshaven, haggard and only slightly older men, who stared straight ahead — big-eyed, exhausted and dispirited. Many of the men chewed their mouthfuls with their lips pulled back and their teeth bared, as if taking care lest hard bread might touch their gums or palates. No one spoke or took any notice of the new arrivals in their clean uniforms, or only insofar as they expressly ignored the fact that they were being watched, which introduced a harsh quality into their faces, a ferocity that might have had something to do with shame. One of them, stretching his neck and closing his eyes, groaned briefly and then collapsed back mutely into himself.

The vault behind the food counter was black with soot. The hash-slinger, an amputee, was playing with a kitten, holding out his empty trouser leg to it and pulling it away when the creature tried to claw it. He was sitting on a stool, supervising the women at the stoves: foreign workers, apparently, because whenever they called out to each other Walter didn't understand a word. Bubbles burst in porridge steaming in a pot, fat sausages were frying in a big pan, ham was hanging from the chimney, and golden fish too, but none of that was meant for the ordinary soldiers. For them, coffee substitute was ladled from buckets into mugs, and each portion of food — a half loaf of bread, a tube of cheese and a slice of artificial honey — had to be shared between two men.

'This should ensure the final victory,' Fiete murmured, and followed Walter along the narrow passageway full of potato sacks into the open air, carrying their breakfast.

On the plateau above the valley stood a howitzer, camouflaged with blankets and shrubs; Walter and Fiete sat down on its ammunition boxes and loosened the straps. The sun rose and the haze of early morning fled; only a few scraps of mist still hung on the blackly wooded hills, lightened here and there by the pale green crown of a tree. Between the trees stood guards with carbines in the crooks of their arms; prisoners in striped uniforms scraped the bark from felled fir trees.

'Just look at this landscape.' Fiete dipped his bread in his coffee substitute and winked at Walter. 'Coffin wood all the way to the horizon.'

Since they stopped being able to drink warm cow's milk out of the bucket, or eat cream and curd with stewed fruit, Fiete had grown thinner, paler too, and some of the other men called him 'the pianist' because of his delicate hands; but the square-bashing in basic training had sharpened the mockery in his blue eyes, and his hair, although cut short, still stuck out in every possible direction. 'So who's going to find you if you disappear into these forests? Disappear until it's all over, I mean.'

One of the camouflage blankets slipped and wind whistled in the gun barrel, whose top third was white from all the chalk marks recording downed planes. Fiete had said those last words half into this bowl, wearily, as if in passing, but Walter still looked round cautiously; no one was sitting anywhere near them. 'What's that supposed to mean?' he whispered. 'Do you want to run away?'

Crows, great flocks of them, were flying eastwards, and Fiete broke off a piece of artificial honey. 'Why,' he answered, 'don't you? Would you rather die in battle, in the mud, just before the end of play? Or be taken prisoner by the Russians and spend the rest of your life in a mine at forty below?' He put the sweet substance in his mouth and winked at Walter. 'I promised Ortrud children, my friend. At least three . . . '

Walter chuckled. 'Well, congratulations. But you can't give her those children if you're brought before a court martial,' he replied, and squeezed some cheese onto his bread. 'Just wait a while — you don't know where we're going to be deployed. They might need us here, at base.'

But Fiete rolled his eyes. '*O sancta simplicitas*, as my Latin teacher would say. They've got enough cripples and prisoners to deal with here already, Ata. They didn't drag us across the whole of the Reich just so that we can peel potatoes behind the front. We're fresh fodder, and we'll be fed to the enemy if we don't skedaddle — don't you see that? Or don't you want to see it?'

Walter bit into the grey bread, accidentally grating his teeth. 'You can take your snooty Latin and grease your hair with it,' he said, chewing.

61

'You don't know what will happen. It could all be completely different.'

'Different how?' his friend insisted, and took a sip of his acorn coffee. 'Are the Russians going to make us blinis? That same Latin teacher, as you might recall, also taught us PE, five classes a week of horrible bullying along with cross-country running and boxing, and because he didn't like me I was always sure to get opponents who'd beat me black and blue. You couldn't do a thing with strength, there, Ata, only weakness. So I gave up on sport and allowed myself an hour down at the harbour, you remember?'

'Very clearly. And what was the result? You got thrown out of secondary school.'

Fiete lit a cigarette and gestured dismissively. 'And if I hadn't been, what would I have learned? Lots of crap about Teutonic heroes. We're in for it, believe me. The war's lost. We'd do best heading off through the mountains to Bavaria. The Yanks'll be there soon. Being locked up by them wouldn't be so bad . . .'

The treetops rustled, and Walter thoughtfully shook his head. 'You don't know that,' he said. 'The Yanks put people against the wall too.'

At that moment the roll call whistle of their Scharführer rang out through the corridors. They drained their coffee, buttoned up their coats and ran to the part of the cave where they had arrived. There, where the typewriters still clattered, stood a truck — a battered Krupp that had just brought in some injured men, about twenty in all. Most of them were half-naked and meagrely bandaged, and they lay on bloody stretchers along the cave walls. Some were unconscious, and the greyish yellow of their faces seemed a foretaste of the terrible things to come; others groaned quietly or constantly shook their heads, wordlessly moving their lips.

Carbines on their backs, marching packs and helmets stacked by the tips of their boots, the new recruits lined up behind the Krupp. An old machine gun with a pan magazine was mounted on top of it, and its gunner, in his dirty uniform, with goggles and field glasses dangling in front of his chest, smoked a cigarette and watched them wearily. There was dust even in his eyebrows and stubble, his lips were barely visible, but in his dark eyes, which had doubtless seen more than the young men could imagine, there seemed to be a hint of pity. He turned his face away and took a deep breath.

The Scharführer waved Walter, Harry and Jörn Asmussen forward and gave them their papers. As they had done their driving tests in basic training, they were to help in the supply unit. The others, who were still chewing their last mouthfuls, had to go and sit on the truck, and the Scharführer himself climbed into the front, beside the driver, hung his arm out of the side window and tapped his hand on the door.

Exhaust filled the entrance to the cave and the men sitting crammed together on benches, boxes and canisters rocked back and forth as the Krupp set off; a strangely blurred picture, since most of them hadn't tightened their chin straps, meaning that their helmets wobbled and slipped. Only Fiete was bareheaded, and Walter raised a hand, but Fiete didn't return his greeting, or did so only with a quiet glance, a grave smile, as he tilted his head back and, like the machine-gunner, scanned the blue sky for fighter-bombers.

★   ★   ★

The driving section of the supply column near Pécs — Fünfkirchen in German — was about to set off. Mohács, sixty kilometres away, was already under the control of Tito's people. Along the streets and in front of mountain passes there were large signs bearing the words 'Warning: partisans! Weapons always at the ready!' In the rough-terrain three-ton and six-ton trucks they brought food and ammunition to the front line close to the Danube and brought back the wounded. If the trucks made it back to the former farm that was their base without any new, sizable bullet holes, and if there was nothing that needed repairing, the men would help the doctors and orderlies in the sick bays or fell birch trees and hammer together makeshift crosses.

The Horch, a formerly elegant, now battered four-wheel-drive officer's car, was covered with nets with fir twigs sticking out of them. It had stopped raining, the clouds were drifting further north, sun flashed in the puddles and Walter unbuttoned the leather flap and pushed it down behind the back seat to have a freer view. 'That's what the Germans are like,' said August Klander, a red-haired lad from Hessen who had just come from headquarters and quickly glanced around:

no officers in sight. 'Back home there's not a thing standing, the front is collapsing, Ivan is at our doorstep, but the field post is still on time.'

Smoking, he hobbled around the vehicle and handed Walter a letter, postmarked three days before. In spite of the running ink Walter recognized his sister's handwriting, her little round letters. She had turned twelve that winter, and had begun using little circles instead of full stops. The envelope had been opened, stuck shut again and stamped with the mark of the mail examination office, presumably because there was something between the pages: a photograph with a deckle edge, showing Leni with short hair, and then a finger-length black feather with gleaming blue patches.

The letter smelled of perfume.

My dear Walter, what do you think of my hairdo? Mashka did it for me, a Pole from the bunker. She sometimes helps at home. At first the frizzy bits were longer, but we made the curling tongs too hot, so a few more inches had to kick the bucket. I hope you're in good health. I'm quite well, I'm barely coughing. We have no school now, it's too dangerous, and I'm getting bored at home. But we're not supposed to stray too far from the cellar door. Herbert, Mum's new boyfriend, always smells of chalk and Lysol. He's the fattest man near and far and can't keep his hands to himself, like Dad. But we have a roof over our heads and something to eat, and since the Polish girls have been sleeping in the coffin storeroom he leaves me in peace.

Recently I was in our old street, or what's left of

it. I climbed around among the piles of stones and blubbed. The block warden wanted to chase me away, he thought I was looting. He even had a gun, but I shouted at him. I'm sending you this feather. It comes from a blue jay, and little Micky Berg says it's a symbol of wisdom and courage.

Where Dad's concerned, we still don't know exactly where or how he is. People who have been transferred for punishment aren't allowed to write, we hear. But a card recently arrived from Uncle Oswald, who's been working at the army clothes office in Meissen. He's done some research and thinks his brother might have been deployed somewhere near Stuhlweissenburg on Lake Balaton. That must be somewhere near you, isn't it? He also sends greetings — our uncle, I mean. Everything has healed very well, and he writes almost as well with his left hand as he did with his right hand, only a bit bigger.

Now the lamp is flickering, and I don't know what else to tell you. I hope we won't have to go back down to the basement again tonight. For the time being they aren't allowing girls into the Volkssturm, which I think is a shame. Herbert has just said I'm ungrateful and a cheeky brat. I liked that. So, see you soon! Don't forget to pick up a pen from time to time. Warmest greetings, from Mum too, your Helene

Walter started the car. August put his helmet on, shoved a couple of stick grenades into the glove compartment and pushed a magazine into his sub-machine gun. 'Let's hope the bloody road isn't blocked,' he said, and sank into the passenger seat. He had been in an ambush a week before in which the whole supply column was massacred; after taking a bullet to the hip, August alone had been able to escape from his burning Borgward into the night. 'News from home?'

Walter slowly drove around the steel tank traps and avoided the puddles as best he could. They'd been given the mission of collecting three paratroopers from the mill in Brevda, a village on the edge of the mountains, which had been an ammunition dump until recently. 'Not exactly,' he said. 'My father was a guard in Dachau and got sent down, probation at the front. And now I hear that he might have been deployed somewhere near here, not far from Stuhlweissenburg. Do you know it? Have you ever been there?'

In the pinewood they were driving through there were field hospital tents; they could hear groaning and screaming from behind the tarpaulins, and August shook his head. 'No,' he said, 'and you wouldn't want to know it either. It's pretty hot there. What did your old man do wrong?'

Walter turned the corners of his mouth down. 'Apparently, he gave some cigs away to camp prisoners. Which doesn't really sound like him. He's always been a tight-fisted, violent bastard. Back when he was unemployed and knocking back schnapps like it was water, he would often come to my bed in the middle of the night and say, 'Why aren't you asleep?' And I *was* asleep. But he was pissed and wanted to fight. He would sit down on a chair nearby and growl, 'If you don't go to sleep straight away you'll get a thrashing.' I could smell his breath and would pray to all the saints . . . '

At the edge of the forest Walter stopped the car, took the field glasses out from under the dashboard and peered out across the horizon. 'But eventually,' he went on, 'I would be shaking with fear — I was still a kid — and he'd see it, and pull the blanket off me, and shout: 'You moved! Now you're going to find out who you're dealing with!' And then things would get nasty. By God, did they ever. With a broom or a poker, until he broke the skin. And he'd get wilder and wilder the louder I screamed.'

'And your mother?' asked August. 'Or your sister? Didn't they say anything?'

Walter put the binoculars away and steered the car out of their cover. Half-tracks stood along the road, blown up or burned out; on some of the mudguards they could still make out a white K, the tactical sign of Panzer Group Kleist. 'Even my mother was scared, even though she's taller than him and twice as broad. I assume she crept under her feather bed. At any rate, she slept with wax plugs in her ears. And my sister was mostly in hospital.'

Water trickled from the rocks, thin streams that scattered when they hit outcrops. August puffed out his cheeks. 'Pff,' he said, 'nice family you've got!' His own parents were teachers in Paderborn, and he wanted to study geology after the war; there was always some mica or diorite rattling around in his gas-mask case. 'Still, there

68

must have been something decent about your old man? Handing out cigarettes in a camp . . . It's almost heroic.'

Walter turned into the road for Brevda. The sign warning about partisans could hardly be read for bullet holes. 'I don't know,' he answered. 'There was often something dark, almost crazy, in his eyes. He liked slaughtering pigeons in his own special way. He held them tenderly with one hand and pressed a needle into their hearts with the other, with the tip of his thumb. And then he let them flutter about in the loft until they were dead.' The road became steeper, and he shifted down a gear. 'Which could take quite a long time.'

★ ★ ★

After they had been driving for three quarters of an hour the windmill came into view. The tip of its tower had been shot away and only scraps of canvas hung from the blades. Walter stopped the truck by a wayside cross and again looked through the field glasses. There wasn't a soul to be seen, not even a dog or one of those thin goats that had been climbing around weeks before, nibbling at the faded thistles on the rocks. The gate was in ruins, the stables were nothing but a pile of rubble and even many of the old olive trees along the wall were charred or in splinters. August released the safety catch on his sub-machine gun.

A soldier with a protective overall over his uniform came out from behind the house and waved. He wore an SS forage cap and a brightly coloured neckerchief, and Walter, exhaling in relief, drove up the road and turned into the farmyard. The three paratroopers, all older than their rescuers, late twenties or early thirties, were sitting at a table in front of the barn, scooping preserves out of big jars. 'Where the hell have you been?' asked the senior officer, a Rottenführer, in a tone of pure pique. 'We've worn our arses out waiting!'

His cheeks were sunken and his nose a piece of flesh-coloured Bakelite. The paratroopers had gone days without shaving. A schnapps bottle, half filled with plum stones, glittered in the sun as Walter turned the car around by a dome-shaped bread oven and called, 'Heil Hitler! Sorry. We were only sent out an hour ago.'

In the rear-view mirror he saw the owners of the farm; they were standing in the open barn. Walter got out, saluted and held his orders out to the Rottenführer, but the man ignored the pages; he ate a piece of cheese from the blade of his knife, studied red-haired August, who had hobbled to the well to fill his bottle, and said, 'Shame he's not a girl, don't you think?' He ran his tongue over his teeth. 'What's that thing they say? Rust on the roof, wet in the basement.'

The others, both Sturmmänner, laughed, and Walter put his papers down on the table and turned round. Striped by the light that fell through the cracks in the board, the old miller, his blind wife and a hunchbacked goatherd stood in the middle of the barn, held rigid atop the

70

blue stools on which Walter usually saw them sitting by the bread oven, holding their glasses of tea. Faces grey, lips cracked, they kept their eyes closed and didn't seem to notice Walter as he went and stood right in front of them.

The black headscarf of the shivering woman, who was clawing her toes into the straw-stuffed seat, was rimmed with salt, while the men's trousers were both wet at the crotch. The wires with which their hands had been tied behind their backs cut so deep into their swollen skin that they could barely be seen. Some of their fingernails had burst from their purple beds, and the nooses around their necks were very tight, though still more or less allowing them to breathe. The ropes hung from a beam under the corn loft, which was empty at this time of year: a high-ceilinged room that echoed with the cooing of doves.

The hunchback, with his chin close to his throat, snorted loudly as if he were sleeping standing up; he also looked completely acquiescent. The miller, too, still wearing his clogs, seemed to have lost his mind long ago; a fly ran over his unmoving face. But when his wife's shaking suddenly became so strong that one leg of her wobbly stool beat against the stone floor, he opened his toothless mouth: 'Zsuzsa!' more groaned than spoken, to which she didn't reply; but it did seem to give her new strength. With dried tearstains on her cheeks, she raised her head and wheezed.

Someone outside clapped his hands. Walter looked round, and now he recognized the

71

kerchief around the neck of one of the paratroopers. It was made of yellow silk with blue flowers and belonged to the couple's daughter; a thirty-year-old widow who had hung a cage full of song-birds beside the gate every morning. Covered with little mother-of-pearl shingles, the cage lay empty and crushed in the rubble. 'So . . . ' said the Rottenführer and got to his feet. 'Eaten enough? Everyone ready? Then let's go!'

He stuffed his spoon into his boot and folded up a map. Like most paratroopers, he also wore a smock known as a 'bone bag' over his uniform: short trouser legs and big pockets. August screwed the cap back on his canteen and asked, 'What's up with those people?' The officer turned round. His right sleeve was brown with dried blood. 'What people?' he asked. Frowning, he looked to Walter: 'Who does he mean?' And when Walter pointed behind him with his thumb, the Rottenführer spat and said, 'Oh, them . . . No idea. They've been standing there all night. They're probably waiting for someone.'

Laughter rang out from the stove. One of the Sturmmänner, bald, brought his canvas bag to the car; grey parachute silk spilled out of it. 'They don't eat anything, they don't drink anything, they don't even get tired,' he said admiringly and opened the boot. 'I'd have toppled off the stool long ago.'

The other Sturmmänner stowed their bowl-like helmets and their knee-pads and set their weapons — three MP 28s with magazines sticking out to the side — on the back seat of the

Horch. 'They're spies,' he explained. 'They haven't a drop of dignity — look at them. They shit and piss where they stand. You can shoot them if you like!' He held a pistol out, but Walter turned back to their superior. 'With respect: they aren't enemies,' he said. 'I know them, Rottenführer, we were quartered here recently. It's the miller and his blind wife. Their daughter, Boglárka, was married to an ethnic German, a Danube Swabian, who fell outside Budapest. She cooked for our whole platoon. And the other one herds the goats.'

The officer, with a straw between his lips, raised his chin and narrowed his eyes. 'I'm sorry — is a driver trying to explain my duties to me? Where are the goats around here? Do you see any goats?' He pointed to the house with the shattered windows. 'I can show you what they've got in the basement, son. If he's a miller, I'm a monkey's uncle.'

Then he put the map in the leather bag hanging over his chest and looked around for his men. 'Right then, damn it, we need to get going. Get the rest of the schnapps out of the kitchen and let's set those birds fluttering!'

The wind exposed the silver sides of the leaves in the trees, and again a discreet 'Zsuzsa!' was heard. The bald soldier lit a cigarette. 'How old are you?' he asked Walter, resting a hand on his shoulder. 'Seventeen? Eighteen? Fresh out of school, right? You don't have a mark on you yet. Have you ever put someone's lights out?' Walter said no, and the other man frowned. 'Really never? What on earth do they train you kids to do, these days? Bake cakes? Right, come on, I'll show you.'

The soldier pulled a chair into the barn, set it behind the hunchback and climbed on. When he loosened the rope, Fredo — that was the goatherd's name — moved his cracked lips without making a sound; a whitish coating had formed on his half-open eyes. 'When you do this thing, you've got to make sure the knot's at the front,' the paratrooper said, and turned the rope around. 'If it's at the back, he just breaks his neck, which takes two seconds. But here, under the chin, the bastard gets the benefit of it. He's conscious for a long while, and he'll wheeze his life away nice and slow.' He grinned at Walter. 'You owe your victims that, at least.'

Climbing down from the chair, he gave his audience a challenging nod, but Walter stayed at the barn door, his arms folded in front of his chest. 'Good God, what sort of victims are you talking about? They aren't partisans!' he repeated, throat dry, voice thin. He gulped. 'They're ordinary civilians, nice people, they let us sleep in their living room. And they treated our wounded and fed the transport animals! You can't just kill them!'

Then the other soldier, the one with the scarf around his neck, shouldered Walter aside and said, 'That's enough of your opera singing! You're inches away from crying, you know that? Partisans, Jews, who cares? What, you never heard of martial law? So off we go, one each . . . '

The stool, the wobbliest of the three, shattered into pieces when the soldier kicked it out from

74

under the miller, and for a moment it looked as if the man, who let out a cry of terror, was about to fall forwards, all the way to the stone floor, his white hair suspended in space. But then the rope gripped his neck and pulled him back into a vertical position with a violence that seemed entirely out of proportion to the delicate old man — as if some invisible force somewhere above the corn loft was jerking him upwards. It was only when the body had stopped bobbing and began to spin on its axis that the clogs slipped from its feet.

The wood clattered loudly against the concrete, and the hunchback, with his eyes firmly closed, was already dangling. A gurgling and groaning came from his thick neck, his bare feet sprinted through the air, and the bald Sturmmann, still clutching the stool, looked for a moment with interest into the dying man's distorted face, the expression of which would have made you think less of a hanged man than of a whining child, in spite of all the stubble. The soldier clicked his tongue with disapproval and said, 'Don't be so greedy, man! Let go. Let go of everything . . . '

But Fredo didn't want to die, and it was probably his hump, the hardened vertebrae, that prevented the noose from closing his airway completely. Twitching, Fredo gritted his teeth as his feet, racing faster and faster, sought purchase. Snot bubbled from his nose, and the soldier threw the stool out of the barn and went and stood in front of his victim. 'Stubborn bastard,' he said. 'Hasn't understood a thing about life, has he? Eventually it's just over, no matter how much of a fuss you make about it. We all have to go.'

With a cigarette in the corner of his mouth he pulled on a pair of gloves and waited for a few heartbeats. Ash fell from the glowing tip, and then it looked as if the broad-backed soldier was hugging the goatherd — which at last he did: ignoring Fredo's drenched trousers, the soldier hugged his hips in two, three violent movements and a backwards tug that made the beam creak, breaking the hunchback's neck.

The doves had fallen silent. Light grey and white feathers floated down from the loft and whirled up again in the breeze, and the two Sturmmänner looked to Walter. 'That's all there is to it,' the bald one said with his hands on his hips. 'No big deal, is it? Kind of thing you should do at least once in your life. Come on, the woman's yours.'

Fredo now hung motionless, with a trickle of dark blood at the corner of his mouth, and even though the Sturmmänner were senior in rank, Walter tapped his forehead — a quick and instinctive movement. His hand shook as he did so, and he turned round and walked to the car. 'Oho!' called the man with the silk scarf. 'So we've got a choirboy here. Won't sully his spotless soul. I don't suppose you do confession? Fine, as you wish, the old woman can stay where she is. Leave her for the rats.'

Shots could be heard in the mountains, the echo of fighting in the valley. After all the parachutes, bottles and ammunition bags had finally been stowed in the boot, and the men had sat down on the back seat beside their superior officer, Walter turned the key in the ignition and looked in the rear-view. Smoke was rising from the house, and the Rottenführer was polishing the stock of his sub-machine gun with his sleeve and blowing the dust out of the holes in its barrel jacket, making a fluting sound. They had left the blind woman as she was, suspended between the two hanged men, with blood running from their eyes and shit and urine dripping from her feet. Shadows on her sunken lids, her grey face wrinkled, the woman tilted her head and moved her lipless mouth — or was she only trembling? The legs of her stool wobbled, and Walter could hear her calling quietly, again and again, not at all urgent or frantic, but as she had probably done all her life — as if her husband were just in the next room: 'Kristóf?'

Her voice was surprisingly bright, almost girlish, and Walter shifted into gear and drove into the road. The suspension of the heavy car groaned. 'Women have all the luck,' the officer said. 'Her partisan pals are probably waiting somewhere in the bushes, and they'll fetch her down in a minute, so that she can make goulash for them . . . ' He leaned forward and tapped the triangle on Walter's sleeve, which identified his corps. 'Listen, noble Samaritan, there's something I've always wanted to know: why do bright, strong lads like you go running around with the light-blue guys? Why are you bringing bread rolls to the front rather than fighting with the troops?'

Walter shrugged and said nothing. He drove

through a puddle, the axle banged, water splashed up before the wayside cross. 'Well, because we've got our driving licences,' August answered for him and scoured the sky with the field glasses. 'Even in wartime, traffic from the right has right of way, Rottenführer.'

The officer laughed, a barking laugh, and smacked August's helmet with the flat of his hand. 'Not bad, son . . . You're pretty smart, aren't you? A student or something, I saw that straight away. But they'll rip you a new arsehole along with everyone else. How are you fixed up at the farm?'

August glanced quickly over at Walter, and he shifted into the next gear and said, 'Supply position A, military hospital operation. There are beds for the senior ranks. It used to be one of General Black's command posts. In the former library at the manor house there's an officers' mess, complete with samovar and easy chairs. And you can play billiards too.'

'Good Lord!' cried the other man, removing his prosthetic nose and shaking it out in the breeze. Silver clips protruded from the hole in the bone. 'Did you hear that? That's how the supply troops live! We're knee-deep in the guts of our enemies and they've got beds! And books! Ah, wouldn't it be nice to lose ourselves in a good book? I've always been a big fan of Karl May. Winnetou's pupils are keener than a hawk's.' He fixed his prosthesis back on, put a cigarette in his mouth and asked casually, 'But listen, boys, if you're so well equipped, enjoying all that luxury, why do you need that old stool so badly? Why are we dragging it along behind us?'

Walter, frowning, braked abruptly and turned his head to look. August pushed his helmet back. The bald Sturmmann scratched the fuller of his bayonet clean with his thumbnail. The one with the handkerchief gazed wearily into the landscape. Their superior officer sparked his lighter.

The old woman's stool, only three-legged now, lay a few metres behind the car in a puddle, and Walter tried to take deep breaths as he got out of the car and walked to the tow hitch. His knife was blunt; he bared his teeth as he cut the rope, and blinked into the sky, where a thin stream of smoke was drifting westwards, but from down here there was no longer any sign of the barn, just part of the mill tower; its shattered roof, in which the wind was ruffling the breast-feathers of the pigeons.

★   ★   ★

Dear Liesel, I hope you got my last letter. I've been waiting for your mail for a while, and if you wrote to me in Hamburg-Langenhorn I'll probably have to wait a bit longer. We're in the field now, in Hungary, I'm not allowed to tell you the name of the town. But I don't have to go to the front line. I'm currently driving a Henschel and bringing supplies to the soldiers. The wine here is good and cheap, forty pfennigs a litre, and everyone drinks all day, even the drivers. In the Puszta it looks like back home, mostly flat, but there are mountains too, and things happen there that I'd rather not talk about. That's what war is like. The locals are on our side, many speak German. They even have a Hitler Youth and a BDM, and if you ask the girls what that means they say 'Boy, Do Me'. But don't worry, I'll be true to you. You be true to me too. You can get the piece of lavender soap out of my room before it dries out, Thamling won't mind. They have lovely blouses here, with brightly coloured embroidery, write and tell me your size. My field post number is now 47704.

Don't smoke too much, it makes your teeth grey. And again: One, two, three. You know what that means.

★ ★ ★

They ran and hid wherever they could as soon as they heard the sound. When the low-flying planes with the red stars on their wings fired their guns, it sounded like someone quilting cardboard: as if strips of pasteboard were being drawn through a Singer sewing machine. They were single-engine Ilyushins, painted a dull, dark green, and only the experienced onlooker could tell that they were now flying with an extra gunner who could also lay down fire to the rear. Until this lesson was learned, many of the relieved survivors who emerged from cover as soon as the shadowy crosses had passed them by were seen to sink abruptly to the ground — often a heartbeat before the machine-gun noise even reached them.

By now reinforcements were stationed in Tata — Totis in German — in the basements of the massive fortress, and every night the supply group drove over the mountains bringing food, fuel and ammunition to the Schambeck Plain. Despite the fact that ground ambushes in this area were nearly non-existent, there were still enormous losses on those terrible roads, which were bombed by the Russians every day and then repaired every night by army engineers again and again. The mountain passes, barely wide enough for a single vehicle, would crumble away, tipping over the trucks carrying wounded, or simply plunging them into a gorge. Traffic jams often formed, sometimes lasting all night, till the morning, when the oak woods — ordinarily dense but in March still relatively bare — offered little cover from the planes.

Walter drove his truck slowly past the remains of a devastated supply column. Tyres smoked, dead soldiers hung from the cabs, mountains of bread were disintegrating in the rain. He had to brake and reverse repeatedly to manoeuvre the three-tonner around tight bends, sometimes skidding and crashing into trees or cliff walls, which would set off the groaning of the wounded lying on the flatbed behind him. Even though it was cool in the late evening, Walter started to sweat.

The infantryman sitting next to him in the cab — a fair-haired lad with a high forehead and thin lips — held out an open tube. The kid's head and right eye were bandaged, but he could still walk and move both arms. Any other soldier in his situation would have been given a tetanus injection and sent back into battle, but his father, Hauptsturmführer Greiff, commander of the supply unit, had probably pulled some strings. 'No thanks,'

Walter said, glancing at the infantryman's yellow pills. 'Doesn't do my nerves much good. I've tried, believe me. After one Pervitin I was awake for three days. My heart was hammering away somewhere up in the clouds.'

Jochen was the boy's name. He grinned: 'That's the point of the things. They're probably why I'm still alive. If you want to sleep you've got to take Veronal. Want some?'

He took out another battered aluminium tube and again Walter shook his head. Jochen shrugged. 'Unfortunately, the stuff makes you randy,' he confided. 'You take a few Pervitin and you can only think about fucking, even stuck in all this shit. Your comrade's blood spurts in your face, you ram your bayonet into Ivan's belly, and as soon as you can breathe again you're dreaming of bubble-baths and plump arses. Even though it makes you completely numb down there, like an old man. You're in your early twenties and you can't get it up.'

It was getting dark, and when they reached the mountain top Walter turned the headlights on. The strips of light that passed through the truck's headlight covers were just enough to let Walter see the bare minimum in the rain: wreckage, rubble, the edge of an abyss. The rubber on the windscreen wipers had worn away, their bare metal arms scratching the misted glass, so Walter and Jochen were both busy trying to rub the condensation away with their sleeves when the brakes jammed. The heavy Henschel 33 skidded some way across the gravel, ending up at an angle, and Walter shifted into reverse to take the pressure off the eroded brake pads. Even so, the brake pedal wouldn't budge; cursing, Walter turned off the engine.

He shifted into gear and got some tools out of the box. There was a sound of rushing and gurgling in the darkness, water poured across the road in narrow streams. Carrying a carbide lamp, Walter crept under the truck and hammered off the rusty nuts, unscrewing the pipes from the encrusted drums. After he had drained the fluid he started the engine again, and the pedal flapped against the floor of the cab. He drove slowly onwards into the valley, almost without putting his foot on the accelerator, and only in second gear, because he could only stop the truck with the handbrake and the gears now. The engine wailed and a jolt ran through the passengers' limbs.

Jochen pressed his feet against the metal of the dashboard and lit a papirosa. His cigarette holder was twice as long as the cigarette itself and, coughing, he held his head. 'Bloody steppe weeds,' he said. 'Stinks like burning mattresses, doesn't it? We'll soon be smoking these in the camps, if we're smoking anything at all. Have you got any real cigarettes left? Secret supplies?'

Walter knew all about the hidden stores, but only said, 'How should I know? You'd need to ask your dad.'

The boy took another drag, and in the glow of the Machorka tobacco his uninjured eye looked feverish. 'My dad . . . of all people. I wouldn't ask him for a glass of water, the bastard. It's his fault that I've got to walk around with a black eye patch for the rest of my life. I could have spent the whole war on easy street! Army research institute in Kummersdorf, not far from home. My mother wangled that one, she liked me more than him, and that pissed the old fellow off. He was worried I'd go soft, that I'd turn into one of them. Always nice cold showers, raw meat on bread and let me at the enemy, you know the drill. Old school.'

Bending forward, he spat on the floor between his feet. 'He knows Sepp Dietrich and had me transferred. Kampfgruppe Ney — all fat bastards and sadists. That toughened me up, of course. But I turned back into a fairy, even at the front. When you're in fear for your life you see it all rushing past before your eyes, and I wrote to tell him that, too. But now that my mother's dead and our house in Jena is a pile of ashes, he's getting sentimental and clinging to family. I couldn't give a damn, believe me.'

The bend in the road ahead of them had been unevenly repaired, and to bring their speed down Walter shifted into first gear. He struck the stick with the ball of his hand, and the moaning in its ancient mechanism, as well as the sound of tearing metal, made the hair on the back of his neck stand up. 'Where were you fighting?' he asked. 'In Stuhlweissenburg as well?'

'Of course,' said Jochen. 'Mid-February. A hellhole, more than a quarter of the regiment snuffed it. Ivan with absolute air supremacy, and not so much as a fart from our planes. And no supplies either, we ate bloody bread from the breadbags of the dead. And once we'd lost the dump we were told we were unworthy to bear the name of the division. Führer decree: cuff bands removed!' He grunted mockingly. 'He'd probably forgotten that they'd been taken off a long time ago; exactly who was to be sent to the front was going to be kept secret until the actual attack — another order from above. But our Adolf doesn't do things by halves: every enemy must be beheaded twice. Why do you ask about Stuhlweissenburg?'

Walter said nothing. They passed the bend, and when he was about to shift up again the stick wouldn't move, not even with Jochen's help. They both tugged on it, the stem vibrated, kicked away, the gear wheels crunched, suddenly the axis was spinning at idle and they heard the click of broken iron teeth in the gear box. 'Great, that's that,' Walter said, turning the truck off. The strips of light across the bushes ahead of them went out. 'It's going to be a cold night out here.'

He pulled the handbrake. As far as he could see, they had reached the edge of the forest. Jochen wound the side window down. The sound of rain, amplified by the tarpaulin over the flatbed, was deafening. Jochen flipped his cigarette out the window and exclaimed, 'You mean we've got to stay here? In the middle of nowhere?'

Walter looked at his watch, its phosphorus numbers. 'Where's else? They'll send someone if we don't come back, but it could be a while. I once had to spend two nights in the steppes, without any kind of cover. I dug myself a hole.

But in case you were thinking of running, it's twenty kilometres to Totis, a good day's march. There probably aren't many partisans but the area's swarming with military police, the kind who like to pick up stragglers.' He put a finger to his temple. 'They'll show you the way.'

Water poured, foaming, down the slope. Walter got out, walked around the truck carrying a carbide lamp and untied one corner of the tarpaulin. Six men lay on the straw that the orderlies had scattered over the metal truck-bed; one had a splinted leg, another a splinted arm tied to a bar on the back of the truck. Almost all of them turned — heads close-cropped because of lice — when the beam from the lamp fell on them: big eyes in dirty faces, terrified expressions. Walter said, 'We've got engine damage, sorry. Somebody will probably pick us up soon. Chuck us your canteens, there's gallons of fresh water here.'

After he had seen to the men — a bandage had to be retied and shitty straw scraped from the truck-bed — he washed his hands and climbed back into the cab. He adjusted the ventilation, put his lamp under the dashboard. Jochen took a small but ornate glass bottle from his knapsack. 'Russian vodka,' he said, cutting the wax off the cork. 'My last prisoner was an officer. He showed me a picture of his children and gave me this hooch . . . I'd have let him go, all things being equal. He spoke a bit of German. But our dear comrades . . . Forget it.' He handed Walter the flat bottle with its grand decorations. 'Have you got a girlfriend?'

He was sliding up close to him, too close, and Walter lifted his elbow, a mute threat. He sniffed the neck of the bottle and sipped the vodka, but couldn't taste anything. 'Yes, I do,' he said, running his fingers along the Cyrillic letters. 'Her name's Elisabeth, Liesel.' After the next swig, a bigger one, he coughed, and felt a faint burning, a warming stream deep in his chest. 'She lives on the farm where I worked. She fled with her mother from the area around Danzig, and she's cheeky, she is, like a gypsy girl. But she did go to middle school.'

Jochen laughed and dug out a new Papirossa. 'Well, then . . . ' Removing the filter he sank back against his fur-covered knapsack. 'My father was always trying to set me up with one of his colleagues' daughters. He's an architect in civilian life, and probably thought I could take over his company some day. But I hate all that right-angled crap. I tend to live in a muddle at home. I wanted to be a painter, to roam around the world wherever I liked and magic up pictures of whatever pleased me . . . But now I can bury that aspiration along with the rest. Or have you ever seen a one-eyed painter?' He drew on his cigarette. 'So how's your old man? Is he in the forces too?'

Walter nodded. 'He's in the Waffen-SS as well, a camp guard. Last I heard, though, he was in a punishment battalion just outside Stuhlweissenburg. No idea if he's still alive. Haven't heard anything for ages.'

Jochen drank the vodka as if it was water. His Adam's apple jerked up and down. 'Yes,' he said at last, 'I wouldn't get my hopes up too much about that one. The whole area is one big military cemetery. When the tank tracks turn and burrow in the dirt, Russian and German bones fly in the air. But perhaps he'll be lucky, we've just retaken the town. It's actually quite pretty there, old buildings covered with stucco and gold. Except that these Hungarian Germans have a screw loose, at least the men do. They all have little square moustaches and side partings. There's a Hitler in every post office.'

He took a few more quick and greedy drags on his cigarette, crunched on two Veronals and washed them down with the rest of the vodka. The bottle smashed in the darkness, and Walter took a matted blanket down from the luggage net and said, 'My father has a snot mop like that too. But he's never been political, he was just looking for work. And with that moustache he got taken on straight away . . . '

Jochen smiled wearily, pulled off his jackboots and curled up in his coat on the seat of the truck, farting brazenly. He wrapped his arms firmly in front of his chest, and after a few minutes he was breathing so regularly that Walter was surprised when he raised his head once more: 'I liked it best at Balaton,' he said thickly. 'That light over the lake and between the trees . . . There was some peace there, believe me! More powerful than any number of shells!'

Then he fell asleep and Walter turned the light out. Wrapped in his blanket, he sat awake for a few more minutes, listening to the rain. The effect of the vodka was already fading, and the cold was creeping up into his legs. In the dark, the wounded groaned or coughed up phlegm, and once a young, almost childlike voice said, as if asleep, 'Mama, help me.' The soldier who had said it must have been lying directly behind Walter, and seemed to be scratching at the wooden side of the truck, now quietly repeating, 'Why won't you help me?' Walter wrapped himself tighter in the rough material.

It was the sudden silence that woke him. Rain was no longer rattling against the truck, the foaming torrent beside the road had become a smoothly flowing stream. Mist crept up the slope and the countless rectangular fishponds in the valley already had a silver-grey shimmer. Shivering, Walter stretched his limbs and rubbed his face. Jochen was wheezing quietly, his knapsack bunched up under his neck and his blanket drawn up over his chin. He looked peaceful and relaxed; his beautiful mouth — feminine in spite of the stubble — seemed to be smiling, but the pupils beneath his closed lids moved tirelessly. A few soldiers on the flatbed were snoring.

Slowly the horizon took shape. Individual poplar trees and the top of a church tower loomed into the strip of dawn which moved so evenly across the black plain that it had a curved appearance. A thrush perched on the highest branch of a birch tree by the edge of the field and replied to the birdsong coming from the forest. From time to time it flapped its wings or hopped on the spot, which made it look rough or angry, cresting furiously as if it didn't like the echo one bit.

89

In the distance a lone fighter-bomber was heading north. Its engine couldn't be heard from the slope; the only way of telling that its guns were firing was the smoke that rose up here and there. The plane grew smaller and Walter unbuttoned the breast pocket of his jacket, in which there was a tin still containing some cola chocolates, and put one of the triangles in his mouth. The blue-jay feather was in the tin as well; he ran his thumb along the edge, and just as it occurred to him that the bonnet of the Henschel was pointing east, and the windscreen must have been reflecting the morning light — a spark against the damp black forest — the plane turned towards him.

He nudged his sleeping companion, shouted his name, but Jochen didn't react, and Walter jumped out and ran around the front of the cab. Wrenching open the door, he reached under Jochen's armpits and pulled him a little way out. The boy groaned indignantly and lashed out. The reflection of the Ilyushin darted towards them across the ponds in the valley, the engine could be heard now, and Walter gripped Jochen more tightly, wrapped his arms around the woozy soldier and fell back against the slope. The truck's windows burst, and shots riddled its chassis. The perforating rattle was followed by the cold *ping* of ricochets, and the wounded men screamed when two tyres burst and the truck, with a hissing jolt, tilted to one side.

The tarpaulins too had been shredded, and now the red stars on the plane's wings were right overhead. The bomb bay seemed to be empty and Walter and Jochen could see the tail-gunner's boots, the pale fur around the legs: his gunfire ripped bark from the oaks and hacked holes in the gravel of the road, before he too passed out of range, over the Henschel. Jochen tried to get up. Walter, however, refused to let go, twigs and roots hanging from his face, ditch water flowing into his boots, listening after the single-engine plane — which didn't turn. Once it had left the mountain ridge behind, it was quiet again in the forest. The morning mist was gradually departing. Light shone through the pale leaves.

The truck-bed too was quiet. Walter pushed Jochen away and leaped to his feet, tearing aside what was left of the tarpaulins. The ridge pole was bent and the metal-covered planks between the beds of straw had thumb-thick holes in them through which blood was dripping onto the road and mixing there with spilled petrol. None of the men reacted to his shouts; he climbed up and stepped over the contorted bodies. Their eyes were filled with such sudden horror or incredulous amazement that it made them look still awake and alive, but a gravity was already settling over their grey faces, which no longer seemed of this world and so left no doubt. An officer with the new Iron Cross pinned on the bandage tied across his chest was clutching a photograph of a smiling girl in his fist, and after Walter had checked his and every other soldier's necks for a pulse, he broke off the perforated dog tags on their chains and put the loose halves in his pocket.

He climbed down from the bed and took a shovel and a pickaxe from the cab. 'Right, then,' he said, half whispering, as if the dead men might hear him, 'help me dig.' But Jochen didn't reply, didn't even turn round. He stood in the road in his stocking feet, took the tube of pills out of his coat and shook it close to his ear, staring all the while down into the plain where smoke was rising from the chimneys of the peasants' cottages and fish were leaping from the ponds into the red dawn.

★ ★ ★

A week later the first basements and storerooms in Totis were cleared as well. The men from the driving unit were lodged in the houses beyond the moat, but none of the guards on the bridge challenged Walter when he set off in the opposite direction, towards the English Garden. Curfew had begun, and where possible he avoided the road and walked close by fences, bushes or piles of rubble. Silence behind the closed shutters, not a person to be seen.

It had turned cold again; ice rimmed the puddles. Walter could see very well in the dark, he could even see the garden paths between the roads, but he only noticed the motorcycle and sidecar at the last moment, and stepped behind a tree. Quieter than the rain, the soldiers were rolling the bike down the Schlossberg; it was only at the bottom of the road that the driver started the engine, skidding on the glistening cobblestones.

The big iron gate was open; Walter stuck close to the pines, only looking up when there was a sudden noise overhead, a loud twittering and rustling in the sleeping trees of the park. The requisitioned cattle in the pavilions and chapels began lowing, dogs barked, and only then did the air-raid siren sound — the old siren on the tower, operated by a crank. Its sound was amplified by the Burgsee as the big spotlights on Calvary Hill, steaming in the rain, swept the clouds.

Most of the windows of the palm house had been covered with boards. Mossy amphorae that had formerly decorated the roof of the baroque building lay shattered in the gravel. The field hospital was a transit station; anyone who didn't have to go back to the front was sent on after swift emergency treatment, towards Graz or Vienna. Hungarian-German nuns sat in the pillared hall to the front of the building, washing bandages in tubs and smoking; a doctor, his stained white coat open over his uniform, shaving at a mirror, studied Walter mutely. Walter answered his imagined question with a nod.

All the beds and straw mattresses that Walter walked past were occupied. Only a few lamps hung in the big room, which was divided by curtains, and aside from the usual field-hospital smell of gangrene and carbolic soap there was a faint scent of lemons or oranges. White blossoming trees stood in wooden tubs in the corners, there were bright pink and red camellias, and young bananas hung from a palm; the marble floor was heated by the warm springs of the town. Here and there men sat on the floor beside their beds, and when Walter pulled one curtain aside Fiete raised his head and grinned.

There was a new seriousness in his grey-ringed eyes, and his teeth were strangely chalky and seemed to be wider apart than before. His scalp stubbly, his left arm in a sling, he was sitting under a narrow window packed shut with sandbags. Walter reached carefully for his good hand, but Fiete gripped him more firmly and drew him down to his mattress; straw spilled from the stitches of the striped fabric. 'Don't look so disheartened,' he said and snapped a book shut. 'I'm not about to kick the bucket. Didn't you bring flowers?'

He wore uniform trousers and a sports shirt with SS runes, and his scalp was red with raw louse bites, some of them already pustular; his eyebrows had been shaved off, too. Walter pointed to his shoulder, to the clean white bandage: 'Will that get you home?'

Fiete clicked his tongue. 'Come off it! It was just a piece of shrapnel below my shoulder blade. If the wound doesn't get inflamed, I'll soon be usable again. About a year ago that would have been enough to send you home, having treated you and everything. But now . . . I've seen machine-gunners on crutches and one-armed tank drivers!' He opened his canteen and poured something into his beaker. 'And by now everyone knows that this war is completely pointless. Our officers are throwing hand grenades after their own men to get them to attack.' Fiete took a swig and asked, 'So, what brings you here, milk

94

soldier? Aren't you with the transport department?'

Walter, who was starting to feel uncomfortably warm, reached into his inside pocket. 'I should be, yes. But we probably don't have to go out tonight, at least not with ammunition. Our section is redrawing the main battle line, pulling it back.' He looked around. 'Of course we can't call it 'retreating'. They're preparing a big push, that's all, and to do that you have to have room to take a run-up, right?' Winking, he handed Fiete a package. 'Here, instead of flowers . . . I'm afraid I forgot the mustard.'

Fiete opened his mouth, his cracked lips, rubbed his chin. Almost all his nails were gnawed down to the skin, and his fingers shook as he unwrapped the greaseproof paper around the smoked pork chop: a big end piece with herb stalks and juniper berries still clinging to it.

'Dear God!' He tilted his head, inhaled the fragrance of marjoram and bay, and his eyes glistened. 'I always thought that dying was the worst thing at the front,' Fiete said, and looked at his friend. 'But it's not true, Ata, it's absolutely not true. If you're lucky, dying is a snap of the fingers. Barely sleeping and never knowing if supplies are going to get through is much worse. The thought of being slaughtered when you're hungry is almost unbearable. You want to eat your fill before you give up the ghost for nothing at all.' Groaning quietly, he bit into the tender meat. 'That is, I mean, for the Greater Germany, of course . . . Thanks, I owe you one.'

Walter waved his hand dismissively. They

95

could already hear the roar of the Russian Tupolev planes and the hissing quad-cannon that the anti-aircraft unit always fired in heavy clouds; they turned quickly on their own axes. Normally the bombers concentrated on the underground bunkers and munitions factories on the edge of town, but tonight there were direct hits nearby. Each blast made the boards over the windows rattle, made dust trickle from the cracks in the high vaulting painted with clouds and birds.

The nuns ran over and switched off the carbide lamps. Their burners continued to glow for a moment longer, and even though it was impossible in all the noise — the guns firing, the wail of engines, the cries of animals — for a moment Walter thought he could hear the spring under the marble, its quiet gurgle. He took off his wristwatch. 'My father fell,' he said and stared into the darkness. 'In a punishment battalion, not far from here. The telegram arrived the day before yesterday. Maybe he was more of a decent guy than I gave him credit for. But now I'll never be able to tell him so.'

Fiete raised his head. 'I'm sorry,' he said, and wiped his mouth with the back of his hand. 'Not something you'd wish on anyone . . . I've seen a few of those suicide battalions. The poor bastards get sent into the most god-awful messes — all just to distract an enemy machine gun . . . Did you get on with your father? Did you like him?'

Walter puffed out his cheeks. 'Well, he wasn't exactly a role model. He drank and hit me and felt up my sister. But sometimes we went fishing together, in the Ruhr — he had a smoking stove in the basement. And his kites made of lantern paper always flew higher than anyone else's. Once I was able to defend myself we barely spoke. But it's funny — since I heard he was dead, my beard started growing a lot faster. No idea why. Have to shave every day, now. And there's something wrong with me, I'm always scared, really terrified, before we go out.'

Fiete drank some water. His parents had died in the air raids on Hamburg, and he leaned his head against the wall, where his jacket hung on a nail, and said, 'I think that's normal, Ata. And he must have loved you, fathers can't help it. Just like you can't help missing something once they're gone. You're really terrified for the first time, and you cry . . . But eventually it makes you stronger, too.'

The glow of flames fell through the chinks in the boards, and Walter scratched the back of his hand and nodded. 'I wouldn't mind that . . . ' He pointed at the hardback book. 'What's that you're reading? *The Secret City?* Is that allowed?'

Fiete grinned. He swallowed the rest of the pork chop, licked the greaseproof paper and then his fingers. 'Don't worry, chief, they're just poems, they won't overthrow the state. I don't suppose you've got a smoke?'

Shaking his head, Walter flicked through the volume, which had occasional notes in its margin. Then he reached into his pocket and handed Fiete a flat box of Overstolz. 'With best wishes from old Jörn. He might drop by tomorrow.'

Fiete, overjoyed, clapped him on the shoulder and put a cigarette in his mouth. Just as he struck a match — tiny sparks leaped from its sulphurous head — it went quiet all around: a roaring vacuum between two heartbeats in which their eardrums throbbed and their breathing paused. And then a bomb exploded beside the orangery.

A jolt shook the vault, big lumps of plaster shattered on the floor, the nurses screamed. Sheets were pulled aside, iron beds shifted, and those wounded who could still walk dragged themselves through the clouds of dust to the door. Walter jumped up too and helped his friend into his boots. Then he wrapped Fiete's jacket around him, picked up the knapsack beside the bed and looked around in vain for Fiete's coat. 'Stolen,' Fiete mumbled, and went outside.

The sky over the park was bright. The burning air made their lungs ache and their eyes stream. The Russians had bombed the part of the town on the other side of the lake with phosphorus. Stuck to the melting tarmac, soldiers burned up in black smoke. Swathed in flames as if in ragged veils, women ran along the promenade, threw their burning children from the wall and jumped blindly after them. Trees blazed, bells sounded, but the arcing fountains sprayed by the firefighters evaporated before they reached their goal.

The AA cannons echoed over the lake and

from somewhere beyond them the wailing descent of a bomber that had been hit. Countless people rolled in the water, which seethed and hissed and steamed, but no sooner had they emerged and tottered back to shore than the chemical reacted again. The rubbery film on their skin burst into flame on contact with oxygen, a bluish flicker, and whenever these desperate men and women, whose cries rang out more and more shrilly across the water, tried to slap out these flames, the fire only clung to their hands as well, leaving them with no option but to sink back silently into the icy water.

★   ★   ★

The road led below some pine trees towards a small whitewashed church. The windows were shattered, one half of the double doors open. The glow of flames from the city flickered over the church's statues and paintings, and the cattle inside, not even twenty Hungarian greys with dark patches around their eyes, turned their heads. A few pews had been hammered together in the middle of the nave in such a way that each pair formed a manger from which the animals ate brownish silage. There was no straw anywhere; cow piss spattered right onto the mosaic floor and Fiete grimaced. 'Just look at that. Old Thamling would crucify us if he saw such scrawny arses. Have the beasts been milked dry?'

Legs bound, tied each to each, they had only just been clipped; a wheelbarrow of ribbed

99

horns, each a good arm long, stood beside the altar. 'Looks that way,' Walter said, touching an udder. The hair-circled teats of the breed were stumpy and short and had to be gripped with the fingertips rather than the fist. 'Or wait, here's a pregnant one, very pregnant. She'll be calving soon.'

The wooden pails in the improvised mangers between the piles of food were empty but too dirty for use, and in the tabernacle there was nothing but a box of matches. Still, the shell-shaped basin of the font was removable, and once he had checked the pregnant cow's fetters, Walter pushed the artfully carved tin bowl under her udders.

Unlike many cows in her condition, which buck and kick out when you take the first milk from them, the milk that is crucial for their calf's survival, this one was behaving very calmly; it even licked Fiete's hand. Walter milked off a good litre, and then the two soldiers sat down and drank from it in turn beneath the Eternal Light that hung from the ceiling. The colostrum was thick as custard and run through with fine threads of blood — there's nothing more invigorating — and after they had emptied the bowl they contemplated the emblem on the floor: a gryphon with a sabre in one claw and three roses in the other. *Fidelis ad mortem*, it said underneath. 'Faithful unto death,' Fiete translated. 'Sounds sort of familiar, doesn't it?'

The guns had fallen silent, the bombers could no longer be heard, but the all clear still hadn't been sounded. 'Ortrud wrote,' Fiete said and looked, smoking a cigarette, through the open church door. Even the reeds were burning; corpses drifted in the water, turned slowly in the current of the feeder streams. 'They're all at their wits' end, too. The pub took a direct hit, the boat is gone. But they're all safe. And now my girl's thinking of a long distance wedding. Had no idea there was such a thing. At the register office they put a helmet on the table, and that's you.'

He edged closer, and even though there wasn't another soul in the room he lowered his voice. 'How would you get away? What do you think? On a motorbike or something? So you can go in any direction you like?'

But Walter said no. 'I wouldn't get away, at least not here. The roads are muddy, it's all flat as far as the border, there's nowhere to hide. The military police see everyone from a thousand metres away and they'll hang you straight away, no trial. They're real bastards. It's probably less risky if you just stay put and try to keep your head down till the end.' He pointed at Fiete's arm. 'Rub dirt in your wound — you might get fever and chills and then you'd be unfit for service. What some people do.'

Fiete plucked something from the carpet on the altar steps. 'And that, ladies and gentlemen, concludes our segment on 'How to Have a Happy War'.' His sombre voice made him sound like a cinema advertisement: 'Rope too tight for you? Bullets too fast? Then why not try lovely sepsis! Three weeks of convulsions in a sickbed, nice and warm in your own shit, and at last you'll hear the angels singing. Free to party

101

members, and for regular people it's available for the low, low price of one human life.'

Walter grinned, waved the smoke away from his face. They both looked up as they heard the pews move beneath the rood loft, heard hoofs scrape across the floor and saw the half-naked figure of a saint, pierced by arrows, wobbling on its plinth. Again and again the animals shoved their muzzles into the empty buckets and Fiete, with a sigh, got up, struck a match and opened the door beside the confessional. The matchlight flame glided along a shelf full of chalices, cruets and other Mass paraphernalia, and suddenly there was the sound of something falling over, and he called out, 'There's a toilet in here, but no water. Not even the holy stuff.'

Walter got to his feet and buttoned up his coat; the steppe cattle turned their heads when he reached for the handles of the wheelbarrow and tipped their long horns on the floor. Slightly curved, they rolled with a bright tinkling sound and came to rest beneath the pulpit; the noise hurt Walter's teeth. He collected a few of the dirty buckets and hauled them in the barrow across the meadow outside, to the shore. The wide beams of the searchlights crossed the sky, and little individual flakes floated down from above; Walter took them at first for snow, but it was ash. After he had tried the water and cleaned the buckets, he scooped them full, put them in the wheelbarrow and wheeled them carefully back into the church. He had also hung two on the handles, though it wasn't until he got to the polished door-sill, more a dip than a bulge, that some of the water slopped over and spilled.

Fiete, wrapped in an embroidered cope, raised a wine glass to him. 'The blood of our Lord,' he said. 'To the Eternal Father, the Prince of Peace and the calf's liver sausage! Not a drop for the dolts!' He had found and lit several thick altar candles; the gold leaf of the icons shone as Walter gave water to the animals, whose eyes were already sunken with thirst. The long shadows of their eyelids lay like tear-trails on their pale grey cheeks; again Walter pushed the wheelbarrow to the lake.

After all the cows were watered, he joined his friend sitting on the altar steps. Cigarette in the corner of his mouth, Fiete held a bottle out to Walter, 'Early Mass Riesling', and they looked out mutely into the night. Sparks burst from collapsing roofs and windows; the air smelled of charred Bakelite. Fire engines and ambulances drove along the opposite shore. Burn victims were wrapped in blankets. Distant cries echoed in the body of the painted organ. 'Elisabeth hasn't written for weeks,' Walter said and sipped at the wine. 'Since we left. I hope nothing's happened.'

★ ★ ★

In the room that he shared with four other drivers, the storehouse of a former bakery, it was still dark when someone called his name. The light from a lamp grazed the white tiles and Walter sat up. Dawn was already breaking behind the silhouette in the open door — a hint of red — and the Junker in the coat said in a low voice, 'Come on, get dressed! We're going to see the boss.'

The cigarette butts on the cobbles were the only sign of where the machine-gun post had stood. The sandbags were in the moat now. Walter buttoned up his shirt and jacket as he followed the man across the bridge. Lorries, some camouflaged with nets and branches, came towards them, and in the courtyard half-tracks were being loaded. Both SS and Wehrmacht soldiers carried boxes, furniture and rolls of carpet out of the fortress, and when someone bumped a big map of the front stretched over a panel against a pillar, little red and green flags trickled to the ground.

The baronial hall was well heated. Hauptsturmführer Greiff, as always in riding breeches and polished boots, was standing under the high bay window, signing a list held out to him by a nurse. He was gaunt, with a sharp profile; the folds and wrinkles in his face had grown deeper over the past few weeks. In spite of the blade-shaped shadow that the peak of his cap cast over Greiff's eyes, Walter thought he recognized a hint of amusement in them when he put his fingertips to the seams of his trousers and clicked his heels together.

The nurse left, and the officer stepped to the big table on which his files were stacked in big folders. 'Urban, correct? Walter Urban, transport department. Where were you last night?' he asked, and studied Walter's dirty uniform. 'As I

104

hear it, you left your quarters without permission. And presumably you know what that means? Three hours of punishment exercises for the whole barracks. At least three — the SS-Stabsscharführer will decide. Under all that nice barbed wire . . . Your comrades are going to love you for that.'

He grinned thinly, and when Walter took a breath to explain his absence, the Hauptsturmführer swept his hand through the air. 'Fine, let's forget that one — you're here now. At ease.'

A loud crackling came from the stove beside the Hauptsturmführer's desk, green and decorated with gold crenellations, and he opened a folder. 'My son told me what you did for him recently, and what he owes you. Or what I owe you, one might say. In fact, your behaviour was simply in line with your duties, only what was to be expected, but in the present situation, when everyone just wants to save his own arse . . . Well . . . At any rate, I'm proud and glad to have men like you in the unit, spirited men, and will recommend you for a decoration.' He tore up a few pages from the file. 'Any objections?'

Commands issued from the corridor, curses and footsteps hurrying down stairs, and at first Walter shook his head, unable to find any words. Then he pressed his thumbnails firmly into the tips of his little fingers, returned to attention and said hoarsely, 'Well, if you'll permit me . . . I don't want to seem ungrateful, Hauptsturmführer, I really don't. It's a great honour. But perhaps . . . I mean . . . ' He swallowed. 'Couldn't I have a few days' leave instead?'

105

With vertical wrinkles between his eyebrows the officer raised his chin. 'You want what?' He laughed drily, as if after some biting witticism, and opened the next folder. 'Secret Command Document', read its cover. 'I'm sorry, son, that's really not an option. You can see what's going on here. You're more likely to get the Knight's Cross. No one is allowed to go home, not even me.'

'No, no!' Walter said quickly. 'I wasn't thinking about home leave, Hauptsturmführer. Everything's destroyed back home, and there are hardly any trains running.' He cleared his throat. 'My father fell recently, near Stuhlweissenburg, and I'd like to visit his grave. I mean, I mightn't even find it. But I would like to have looked for it.'

Engines were starting in the courtyard; the window panes vibrated. The officer studied Walter once more, now with a mild, almost civil expression on his face, and pulled his gloves on. The thin leather was so tight that you could see every knuckle and even his double wedding ring. With a shake of his head he opened the stove door and pushed some papers inside. A whistle rose up the chimney, flames darted from the door, the yellow pages turned black and the big SS runes white in the fire before everything turned to ash.

Then Grieff sighed audibly, reached into his desk drawer and uncapped his pen. 'Fine,' he said. 'Just this once. This is a marching order, Stuhlweissenburg and district. Don't say a word to anyone. Go to the motor sergeant and tell him

106

to issue you with a vehicle and fuel for three days. No detours, no contact with the population. After that I want to see you again in Abda, where we'll be moving temporarily. It's southwest of Gyõr on the Raab, ask around.' He handed Walter a document with a wink. 'And don't forget your carbine. As far as the Russians are concerned we're criminals even when we're on leave.'

Walter saluted. The cushioned door fell shut. There was no one on the stairs now or in the offices, the open cupboards were empty; he ran across the courtyard, where only a limousine with blue flags, an Opel Blitz truck full of fuel canisters and two motorbikes were parked. The Schirrmeister, a fat reservist whose office was in the cellar of the keep, was putting his helmet on as Walter came in, and said, 'You should have come earlier, lad. Where am I supposed to conjure a car from? Two Stoewers and a Kübel of mine were shot up last night, nearly brand new.' He spat. 'I could offer you a little donkey or a requisitioned lady's bicycle. Or you could take one of the messengers' boneshakers out there. They've got full tanks at least.'

The four-stroke bikes — a BMW R75 and a Zündapp, both with sidecars — were encrusted with mud, but their engines sounded impeccable, and after Walter had checked the oil and the tyre pressure, he opted for the BMW. He took a fuel canister from the flatbed of the Blitz, tied it on behind the spare wheel and drove slowly over the bridge to his quarters to fetch a coat, his field kit and some supplies. The March

107

sun shone brightly over the town. Charred corpses lay amid the few remaining houses but the fires had gone out and the lakes of phosphorus in the market square were now scattered with sand. Spit-cakes and fresh sesame rings were already on sale again. Most of the Reich flags above the doors of the houses hung in tatters from their poles.

★ ★ ★

By the entrance to the English Garden, with its yellow forsythias, two military policemen stood smoking in open capes. On the polished granite cobblestones the braking distance was longer than usual, and Walter hadn't skidded a bike's length past the man with the red signalling disc before the other one had released the safety catch on his sub-machine gun. Walter raised one pacifying hand, reached the other into his coat and held out his pay book and marching orders to the policemen. The tips of its pages trembled, and the officer with the gun studied Walter with narrowed eyes before he looked over the documents.

'Oho!' he said. 'Someone's in good with the boss. From the man himself . . . But here it says Stuhlweissenburg, soldier — that's *towards* the gunfire, not away from it. Or are we actually looking to desert, when all's said and done?'

Walter's jawbone twitched. 'No, no, why would I do that?' he answered and pointed to the park. 'I'd just like to say a quick goodbye to my friend. He's in the hospital.'

The officer looked past him at the main road, where a troop of prisoners was marching; bearded Russians in the rags of their uniforms. Some were barefoot, and the Hungarian-German militiamen who were guarding them seemed to enjoy cracking their whips. 'In the palm house? Nothing in there but corpses now. All wounded men still capable of travelling were taken to Gyõr early this morning. And by the way, soldiers don't have friends, they have comrades.' He threw the papers onto his tank. 'Now wipe that sweat off the back of your neck and clear off!'

Walter saluted and left the town heading south. The land was flat all the way to the horizon, the previous year's grass crushed by the rain. Here and there a wellhead which cast blue reflections in puddles and hoof-prints. No people anywhere, no cattle, but between the burned or derelict cottages along the road there were tilled fields. Young maize shimmered over crumbly soil; even tank tracks had been used as furrows; turnip leaves on red stems emerged from mulched straw.

A buzzard sailed high above the bike, the feathers at its wing-tips spread. Walter stopped under a tree and unscrewed the lid of his canteen. In the bird's repeated calls he thought he heard shrill outrage at his presence; only as he drank did he notice the rabbits, a dozen or more. They lay motionless, far apart in the brown grass; anyone would probably have looked right through them had it not been for the quiet wind that ran through their fur from time to time, showing the white skin beneath.

Their ears flat against their backs, their back legs outstretched, they quivered at the cry of the buzzard whose shadow began to move faster over the grass, flying in circles, but the rabbits gave no sign of fleeing or seeking cover. They were all so thin that their ribs showed, and their eyelids were swollen nearly shut — what little eye could be seen in those slits looked bloody. Walter scoured the plain with his field glasses. Then he hung his gas mask on the handlebars and rode slowly on.

It came from the east, the wind, you could imagine you smelled mountain herbs on it, and the sun was already high in the sky when he reached a hamlet in the Puszta — four or five houses with roofs of rusting metal, a single great chimney looming over them all. The chimney belonged to a tile factory, now abandoned; the kiln was cold, the wooden moulds empty, and tender green stems grew from the mud and clay mixture in the middle. The cottages seemed just as abandoned, their shutters closed, and when Walter tried the bell pull by a door only the hinge squeaked. The bell had no clapper.

From an oak by the crossing, where a whitewashed bakehouse stood, a hanged man dangled — a soldier of the Waffen-SS. His hand was thickly bandaged and his face — eyes narrowed and mouth open — was covered with dust from the road. He might have been Walter's age. On his cheek, which almost touched his shoulder, Walter could make out beak marks, and on the man's chest there hung a white

110

wooden sign with the inscription 'I am a COWARD. The same will happen to all traitors to the Fatherland who abandon their comrades. VICTORY OR SIBERIA!' The neat, level letters, which looked as though they had been professionally printed in black gothic script, were painted on the sign along pencil lines.

No insignia now, no identifying marks; Walter took the camera out of the sidecar, a little Voigtlander in a leather case that he had borrowed from Jörn; but then he couldn't bring himself to click the shutter. He went into the bakehouse and sat down on a bench under its little window. Pillars of smoke, far apart, rose into the sky on the horizon and combined to form an extended black cloud that was drifting towards Lake Balaton. Walter could feel the impact of shells as vibrations under his feet; the knot on the tree branch creaked whenever a gust of wind stirred the hanged man. Even the corpse's teeth were grey with dust.

An old beech branch with almost transparent leaves trembled by the crossing; Walter huddled up on the bench. Using his felt-covered flask as a pillow, his hands folded between his knees, he slept for over an hour under his coat. In the afternoon he ate some bread with cheese from a tube, filled his bike's tank and set off again along the path, a crooked trail between thorny bushes, grey with tufts of wool at waist height. Young soldiers hung from other trees or posts on the plain, all with large-lettered signs hanging over their chests. Many had had their pockets turned out, hardly any wore boots, and their feet, if they were close to the ground, had been gnawed to the bone.

The shadows grew longer, and after Walter crossed the grassland to a small mound — his trail of dust still darkened the air far behind him — he turned onto a cobbled road. Lined with ash trees, it led into a village with a railway station and a pub of sorts that bore the word 'Wolfen'. He asked the two soldiers by the anti-aircraft gun the way to the cemetery. The 3.7 cm gun was screwed onto a trolley and the men, who sat smoking on the ammunition box, eyed Walter wearily. 'There are more graves here than living people,' the taller of the two replied, a Gefreiter with a bandaged head. 'Who are you looking for?'

The narrow field of honour for the fallen members of the Waffen-SS, surrounded by a fence, lay on the way out of the village, and was distinguished from the graveyard for Wehrmacht soldiers on the other side of the road by the fact that the crossbars of the birch-tree crosses were both set at a downward-facing angle, forming the arrow-shaped death rune. On the crosses' upper tips were the helmets of the dead; Walter turned off his engine, opened the leather-hinged gate and walked along the graves, his heart thumping in his throat. There were small wooden signs with burned inscriptions and here and there flowers lay on the plinths: star hyacinths, yellow cinquefoil. But he couldn't find his father's name.

At the far end of the cemetery stood a particularly large cross — it too was made of birch wood, and the soldier who knelt before it, raking the earth, was looking back at Walter. He was an elderly man, already bald, with glasses and aluminium braiding on both sleeves of his uniform, and he picked up his crutches from the grass and got to his feet. As he did so, he gritted his teeth, but shook his head vigorously when Walter came over to help him. 'What is it?' he wheezed and put the claw-like rake in his bag. 'Can I help you?'

Walter saluted, told him who he was looking for, and the officer read the telegram that had brought news of the death, bearing the battalion stamp. 'No Alfred Urban here,' he said. 'These were all my men. Last week they were singing merrily . . . ' He took a silver case from his pocket and snapped it open. There were slender cigarettes in it and a photo stuck to the inside of the lid. 'I'm sorry to disappoint you, but members of punishment squads seldom get a memorial, son. People aren't going to saw a tree down for that. They're buried where they fall — if at all. And Stuhlweissenburg is a hotly contested area . . . the enemy isn't exactly known for looking after cemeteries, is he?'

The old man offered Walter a cigar, and Walter looked again at the photograph in the case — a family in a garden having tea — then he said thank you, pushed the gate shut and rode on. The land was hilly and the road wasn't bad, it was even paved over long stretches. But farmers warned him of Russian planes, and where possible he sought the cover of the forests or crossed the fields along log roads. Every hundred metres, camouflaged armed reconnaissance vehicles stood between the trees, and the men from the measurement and meteorological branches studied him through their field glasses. With pine sprigs on his helmet and a telephone receiver to his ear, one of them pointed at where he was headed and dragged a warning thumb along his throat. Walter grinned and waved to him.

He searched through several cemeteries that day, getting closer and closer to the front. The last one he encountered before sunset was on the western side of a hill, behind which the fire-flashes of the main battle line were visible — the black smoke. The cemetery's fence had caved in, its ground churned by tank tracks, and bombs and shells had turned the graves inside out: ribs, matted hair, bared teeth in the earth. Rust-coloured water stood in the craters, and Walter held his cap over his nose and mouth as he walked along the rows to read those markings that were still legible. The evening sun filled the helmets on the ground with shade, the wind grew cooler and agitated the translucent bark peeling from the birch crosses, and here again Walter could not find his father's name.

Back on the road of churned gravel, he rode for a while along the ridge of hills that ran parallel to the front. Because of the many wrecked tanks — quite a few of their mudguards bore the white key, the emblem of the Leibstandarte — Walter kept having to dodge into the weed-covered fields. The BMW wobbled on the loose soil, and in the end it got too dark for him to continue. He could hardly see anything in the narrow strip of light from his blacked-out headlight, so he rolled the bike into the ditch.

As the night bombers roared, he collected two handfuls of twigs and lit a fire under the bed of a bullet-riddled Hanomag van to warm up some potted meat. He spooned it out of its tin with a corner of bread and, chewing, looked across to the battle line, where scraps of fog were blowing across the meadows and scattered vehicles burned. There was no sound now of grenade launchers or heavy guns. Sometimes a salvo of machine-gun fire echoed up to him, or a flare rose into the sky and sank smoking into the valley: red, green or white light, beneath which the course of a river glittered and the shadows of individual trees turned. Not a soldier to be seen.

It was getting even colder; Walter smelled rain, and after he had eaten another apple he plucked dry grass from the field, piled it up under the engine block and spread his tarpaulin over it. Using his rucksack as a cushion, he was able to sleep; protected from the low-flying planes, coat buttoned up and all wrapped in his blankets. Smoke drifted up the hill, but the front was calm now apart from the music with which the Russians on the other side of the river were trying to entice turncoats to cross over: 'Homeland, Your Stars' or 'Lili Marlene'.

The music blew away, and Walter must have been asleep for some time before he heard footsteps on the road. Holding his breath, he couldn't tell if the rustling in his ears was steppe grass or the sound of his own blood. He pulled his carbine over carefully and released its safety catch with his thumb, holding his little finger on the wood so that the click wouldn't give him away. He turned his head, but even though moonlight was shining through the clouds he couldn't make out a thing or a person among the wrecks; by now he assumed he'd only dreamed the footsteps.

But then they got louder, the steps: feet cautiously treading or creeping over gravel, and Walter's heart thumped so hard it moved the dog tag lying on his neck. 'Come, comrat! Come! Choclat! Schnapps!' rasped from the loudspeakers in the valley; another flare was lit, and at last Walter could see legs right next to him — the black, gleaming, cloven hoofs, spreading slightly with each step, of a roe deer, whose shadow, with its short antlers, fell at an angle across the road and who seemed to have sensed Walter's presence at just the same moment. The deer snorted roughly, a sound like a death rattle, and, sending soil and small pebbles swirling into the air, it leaped to the side and disappeared in the bushes.

Walter breathed out with relief. He listened to the night for a while longer before securing his carbine, taking a sip from his canteen and going back to sleep.

Towards morning, raindrops drummed on the riddled chassis, water trickled from the engine block, and he pulled the tarpaulin over his head. The cool wind, which brought the sound of twigs grating one against the other, smelled

116

of sulphur and petrol. Someone in a half-sleep said 'sin and Berlin', and at last Walter was awoken by a vague shivering that he thought at first was his own — until he felt the earth itself trembling. It was still dark, a depthless, inky sky, but against the strip of red dawn he could make out the silhouettes of troop transporters and tanks, long columns moving quickly in his direction.

Quaking with cold, he crept from his hiding place, rolled up his blankets and pushed the BMW out of the ditch. He washed his eyes with a handful of water and cleaned his teeth with a handkerchief as the first vehicles made their way around the nearby wood. There were soldiers clinging to every possible surface on the vehicles, some still in winter camouflage, sitting or standing and holding on tightly wherever they could — not only on top of the heavy trucks, on top of the scout cars and the howitzers being towed behind them, but also in the turrets and atop the skirts of the tanks. There were traces of sweat and tears on their dirty faces, and many were wounded; the fresher bandages stood out clearly in the dawn light, and while some of the men drew greedily on their cigarettes, scouring the sky for fighter-bombers, others concentrated on holding pieces of bread and potato, on skewers, to the red-hot exhaust pipes.

Walter started the BMW. He didn't have much room to manoeuvre on the narrow path, and only advanced at a walking pace; sometimes the wheel of his sidecar hovered over the ditch.

Some squaddies frowned or tapped their foreheads when Walter looked up at them, and he had to stop at the next crossing, which was blocked by a tractor. The driver was turning the ignition in vain — he was out of petrol — and everyone who still had the strength jumped from the bed of the stalled truck and ran down the road to climb onto the next, equally overloaded vehicle, though only a few of them were able to find room. Their comrades struck out at them with sticks and crutches and the ones left behind cursed and shouted, bloody hands clutching the air.

Walter, to escape the crush, wanted to turn onto a road across the field, but a roofless Horch broke away from the column and blocked his path. It too held wounded soldiers, and at the wheel was a Wehrmacht captain who said something that Walter couldn't make out over the noise of the engines, the rattle and clink of the tank tracks. But assuming that the captain had been asking where Walter was headed, he pointed east, and the officer, his goggles over the brim of his cap, grimaced and shouted, 'What on earth are you going *there* for?'

Walter handed him his marching orders. 'I'm looking for my father's grave,' he replied, and the man read the papers and shook his head. The column paused and for a moment it was quieter. Everyone was engulfed in exhaust.

'Ivan's in Stuhlweissenburg, son. The only grave you'll find there is your own!'

★ ★ ★

118

Dear Mother, I hope you are all well. I'm in good health, even if the damp cold is often a problem. But now spring is on the way, and there are many blossoms. I'm sitting here in Ròzsa — Rosenort in German — in a little post office, and there's no one else around. Perhaps the people have fled, perhaps it's their lunch break, I don't know. The heroes' cemeteries, where I'm looking for Dad's last resting place, are getting bigger and bigger. The Russians are putting on the pressure, and the ground-attack pilots are shooting at anything that moves, even refugees. If you turn this card over, you'll see what it looks like here in the summer, in peacetime. (But you'll have to imagine it without the tower of the spa, since it took a direct hit.) Thank you for the birthday wishes and the package, I was delighted. I hope we'll meet again soon! Your son

★　★　★

Doves circled above shattered dovecotes. Some roofs were burning, doors and windows were open, household goods and shredded feather beds lay outside doorways. In every street there were teams of horses and oxen, piled high with mattresses and furniture with children sitting among them, but most people were on foot, pulling barrows or pushing bicycles laden with luggage. They made a point of not noticing Walter. Only their dogs barked at him.

The herds were being brought to safety. Dust floated over the corkscrew horns of the Wallachian sheep and the cracking whips of the peasants rang out below the gatehouse. With old rifles on their backs, they wore knee breeches, white shirts and red waistcoats — the costume of the Hungarian Germans in this region — and had already removed their square moustaches. The shaved patches were paler than the rest of their stubbly faces.

Wehrmacht HQ was in the Hotel Rebmann, a half-timbered house in the marketplace of Kiszémel, the town the Germans called Klauben. Military vehicles kept sheltered, close to the houses, and the evening gave a red tint to their windows. Walter drove the BMW into a dilapidated shed and took the spark plug out of its socket. Then he filled his canteen at a well and trudged up the hill behind the burned-out school.

The last cemetery that he came to after another day of fruitless searching was on the edge of some vineyards. The vines had just been pruned and drops of water gleamed where the cuts had been made. The drops were sticky and tasted sweet, and as he licked his fingers he read the names on the few remaining crosses. Where a bomb or a shell had struck the hill, birch twigs were being used to prop up the budding vines. The paths between the rows of plants were paved with gravestones bearing Hebrew inscriptions, and in this graveyard, yellow with crocuses, once more he failed to find his father's name.

In the market square again, he saw from a distance that his reserve petrol was gone, the canister's strap dangling over the ground. Laughter shrilled from the open hotel door; a sergeant with his cap pushed far back into his sweat-drenched hair stumbled over the threshold and threw up. In the corridor and the taproom were drinking soldiers, mostly of higher ranks; Walter skirted around the building's bowed front and looked for another way in. From the narrow, open windows, painted with tar, came the sound of piano-playing and song, roaring, screeching, clapping.

He climbed a flight of wooden steps to the smoky kitchen. Private soldiers and female auxiliaries sat inside at a long table, eating soup. The heat beneath the low-beamed ceiling was intense, condensation dripped from the blue and white tiles, and here too no one seemed to be sober: faces gleamed, voices slurred. Countless stone bottles stood on a side table — German schnapps — and a man with a salt-and-pepper beard, a Wehrmacht quartermaster to judge by his uniform, beckoned Walter over to the stove. 'We've got some beef goulash,' he said, filling his plate. 'Dig in, son! In the camp you'll get nothing but stones.'

An orderly belched and made room for Walter on the long bench. He held out a bottle of wine and a basket of bread, and Walter took off his coat and sat down next to a woman. With her forearms on the table and her cheek resting on the backs of her hands, she seemed to be sleeping, a thread of drool hanging from her twisted mouth. She sat there with her legs spread, her bottom stretched on the edge of the bench, her skirt hoisted to the buttons of her suspenders. Walter smelled a hint of eau de cologne, tore off a piece of white bread and dipped it in the goulash.

It was thick and hot, but the meat was tough, and as he chewed he heard music coming from the next room and only noticed after a while that the woman was looking at him. Without lifting her head, she licked the corner of her mouth and said, 'Yeah, right, another fine promise . . . So, are you all done fighting? It's all over, right? The trucks aren't getting through any more.'

Her hair and eyelashes were strawberry blonde, her eyes weary. Even though she was only a little older than Walter, perhaps in her mid-twenties, she already had fine wrinkles under her eyelids and around the corners of her mouth. 'If only I'd stayed at home, silly cow that I am. Never volunteer for anything, Grandpa always said, the best seats in war and the cinema are at the back. You'll hurt your eyes at the front! But no, I wanted to go out and see the world . . . ' She jutted out her bottom lip and blew a thin strand of hair out of her face. It only floated back. There were tiny freckles on her cheekbones. 'Well, even dying doesn't last for ever, right? You look familiar. Waffen-SS? Have I seen you here before?'

The brass emblem on her sleeve, the lightning bolt of the telephone unit, glittered in the candlelight, and Walter shook his head. 'Not likely,' he said. 'I'm only passing through. I've been looking for a grave, my father's grave. Do you think I could sleep here tonight?'

She sat up with a yawn, pulled her skirt straight and loosened her tie. ''Course, there are more than enough soft beds around here. Used to be a hotel, after all. Famous people used to stay here — Reich ministers, for example. Or Zarah Leander and Willy Birgel — very charming.' Tilting her forehead, she lowered her voice: 'But if you don't play for the other team, I'd think long and hard. For young privates there's only room one-seven-five, a very, very hot and stuffy room. You'll hardly catch a wink.' She pressed her knee against his. 'Did you hear me, young man?'

Walter closed his eyes for a moment and drank carefully from the bottle of wine, whose neck, he now noticed, was broken: suddenly the sharp opening glued itself to his lip and the woman chuckled. 'Greedy enough . . . Do you know what I was dreaming, just now? Shall I tell you?'

Walter shrugged, and the woman drew a crocheted handkerchief from her sleeve. It smelled like her perfume. 'I was working at a beautiful palace, just imagine. Gold and crystal everywhere, and I was supposed to be guarding this sort of jug. It contained the elixir of eternal life, and everyone prayed to it, every Sunday. It was a state job, you see. But despite my responsibilities, I still drank from the jug, and gave the rest to my fiancé, because I didn't want us or our love to die. I mean, it's funny, I'm not even engaged, I don't even have a boyfriend. But the man in my dream had beautiful eyes, like Josef Loibl . . . Wait a second, you've cut yourself.'

She dabbed some blood from his top lip. 'Anyway, I refilled the bottle with water, but somehow someone found out anyway, and we

123

were sentenced to death, just like that. We were standing beneath the gallows, with nooses around our necks, when I said, 'Stop now, stop! Think about it! If that liquid really granted eternal life, you couldn't put us to death! It's impossible! If we die, everyone will be able to see that it was all lies, that the whole cult is just opium for the people! There would be a palace revolution!'' Smiling, she held out the palms of her hands. 'And what do you think happened? They took the ropes off again and set us free!'

Walter exhaled gently through his nose and pushed his plate away; the woman leaned against him, ran her finger through the last of the goulash and licked it. 'Impressive, don't you think? I'm clever in my dreams at least. Couldn't you put your arm around me?'

He stroked her temple, and again she pressed her thigh against his. He could feel the button of her suspender. She reached for his hand, rubbed the damp palm with her thumb, but at that moment the door flew open and an officer in shirt-sleeves, braces hanging from his waistband, stared, blinking, around the room. Piano music, a Bavarian polka, interspersed with whistling, forced its way into the room with him, and he clapped his hands and cried, 'We need more schnapps, damn it! Juniper for the final victory!' Tottering, he pointed to Walter and the young woman. 'Come on, come on, you turtle doves, take a few bottles to the front. But the large calibres, if I may be so bold! So that nothing's left of us, afterwards . . .'

She pulled a face. 'He's homosexual, too!' she

muttered as she got to her feet, and they both took earthenware bottles from the side table and followed the man down the corridor. Old hunting weapons, antlers and stuffed boar's heads hug on the walls of the crammed pub, which was lined with cork to shoulder height. The wax of countless candles dripped from the lampstands — huge cartwheels — and the oven plate was glowing as Walter pushed his way through the crowd and set down a Steinhäger bottle on the sill of a blacked-out window. There were sub-machine guns resting against it as well.

The pianist was naked to the waist, and a young woman in a short petticoat was dancing on a nearby table. With one of those crescent-shaped military police badges on her chest, she wound her way through outstretched arms, knocking over glasses and stepping on plates and trays. The soldiers' fists and knuckles showed under the black silk fabric like the vertebrae of lithe animals, and when she threw her head back, laughing and crying at the same time, her mascara ran into her ear. Beneath the pictures of Hitler and Szálasi in reception, men drank schnapps from each other's mouths and reached under each other's uniforms. From the next room, a billiard room, came the cries of people having sex.

A fat sergeant pushed a dancing couple over the chalk line a good two metres from the stove. 'Next!' he cried. 'She's built up some pressure now! All bets are off!' They formed a circle, and an elderly woman wearing only a pair of suspenders and a soldier's cap put her arms around the shoulders of two squaddies, who reached down to the backs of her knees and lifted her legs up. Her pubic hair, a broad triangle, grew to her navel, and her heavy breasts, bitten red and blue, hung to the sides of her ribs. When she laughed she revealed a gold tooth.

The piano fell silent, and for a few seconds almost everyone was quiet; it was an expectant silence, as the woman stared at the ceiling and gnawed at her lower lip as if trying to concentrate — and already the silence was too long for one major, who dribbled more schnapps into his cup quite audibly. Then the pianist played a trill, and at last the old woman closed her eyes and pissed a bright yellow glittering stream in a high arc onto the plate of the oven, where it steamed with a pop and a hiss. There was a round of applause and cheering, banknotes changed hands, and the smell of burnt urine made Walter gag for a moment. He swallowed a bitter burp.

A drunk man, his shirt drenched in sweat, jostled Walter, slurred something in his ear and felt his muscles, before turning towards the Blitzmädel. Walter left. It was already getting dark outside; he took a breath of the cold air and walked slowly across the courtyard. Between the bins lay a dead officer, a gaunt man with an oak leaf on his collar patch, his gun still in his open mouth. He was wearing new jackboots with Wehrmacht stamps on the light-coloured heel-breasts, and as Walter buttoned up his coat he checked his foot against one. Too small.

Not a soul in the streets, not a dog; he pushed the BMW out of the shed and was screwing the spark plug back in when the Blitzmädel came out of the pub. Her tie with its eagle pin was tied properly again, her hands were in her jacket pockets. She looked into the sky, where the evening start was shining. 'So, are you leaving me alone?' she asked and smiled wearily, closing her eyes for a moment. The skin of her face, still alabaster in the kitchen, now just looked washed out. 'You men are all the same . . . My name is Reinhild, by the way, in case you want to try and remember me. Reinhild Lerche. My family lives in Grainbach in the Chiemgau. We embroider these traditional cloths . . . Did you ever find your father's grave?'

The rhythmic wail of the 'Stalin organs', the Russian rocket launchers, sounded in the distance, only occasionally interrupted by the crash of German artillery. Walter put on his gloves and shook his head; after he had swung himself onto the rubber seat, the woman stepped closer to him. Her milk-blue eyes were clear, her expression alert; she leaned over, keeping her hands in her pockets, and kissed Walter on the temple. She whispered in his ear, 'Stay safe, you hear me?' He nodded, wished her the same thing, a hoarse, 'You too!' and started the engine.

★ ★ ★

He spent the night in a windowless hut on the edge of the vineyards, on a flat raffia bed. The

127

door bolted on the inside, but he could see the sky through the holes in the roof, the white moonlit rims of clouds. The honks of wild geese came from the north. Somewhere an engine roared, and a little later went quiet, this quiet becoming rather overbearing as soon as Walter noticed it.

Willow panniers hung on the wall above him, and he pulled the tough remains of grapes from the weave and chewed on them until they gave off no more sweetness, and no sourness either. Then he spat them out, clasped his hands behind his neck and looked at the furry patches of saltpetre efflorescence on the wall, which looked like the silhouettes of people, same as the ones he sometimes saw with his eyes closed — a sequence of profiles, just their outlines, slipping quickly across his retina, familiar and strange at the same time.

After he had slept for a few hours, he set off again early in the morning, while it was still dark. The air was filled with the roar of Russian bombers flying west at a high altitude, and every now and again an Ilyushin left the squadron and looked for targets in the lowlands. Walter, who had stuffed the sidecar with dry brushwood and tied a straw mat to his back, got through the steppe without being fired at, and in the late morning he reached Győr, where hardly a house had been left undamaged and even the church towers were smoking.

Here too the flight was beginning, handcarts and horse carts being laden with household goods, and Walter drove slowly along a rickety pontoon across the Raab, which smelled of putrefaction. In the grey-green current, corpses drifted in their German and Russian uniforms, spinning in the eddies, disappearing beneath the boards and reappearing on the other side. Some, stiff and swollen, got stuck, and soon trapped any new arrivals among the boats and vessels, which endangered the necessary mobility of the whole enterprise: children immediately came running with long poles and poked the floating bodies free again.

Rain was falling, but the sun shone behind the veil of water. Corpses with bloodstained faces lay on the road to Abda, and when Walter took a turn around the stable building of a farmyard, he found himself facing a long line of haggard men in grey prison uniform marching towards him. They were Jewish forced labourers from the mines in Bor, he was told by a guard on a bicycle at the rear of the column — a Hungarian-German clutching a 'broom handle', an old Mauser. 'We're taking them home to the Reich. If they stumble, they're done for. Don't know why we're still doing this to them.' With his forearms on the handlebars, he spat out some tobacco juice; it dripped thickly from the lamp. 'Why we don't just finish them off, I mean. What do they expect to get out of these scrawny buggers . . . Hey, do you have any schnapps?'

A pair of rusty pincers hung from his belt. Walter said no and rode slowly past the procession. The men, hung with scraps of sacks and blankets, held their stubbly heads low and barely noticed him. Struggling to keep pace, in foot wraps or barefoot, they stared straight ahead apathetically and only gave a start — for some it was hardly a twitch of the eyelids — if, somewhere in the endless row ahead, the strangely toneless report of a nearby pistol rang out, like a hand clapping. Then they straightened their backs, and all marched a little faster.

Just before a signposted fork in the road, Walter reached into the sidecar and handed the nearest man his last tin of sausage. The slender, bespectacled man, whose trouser legs were different lengths, immediately hid it under his jacket and nodded, barely perceptibly, looking neither at Walter nor at the man who had just been shot by the edge of the field — who trembled and convulsed and dug his bare heels into the earth as a militiaman forced his jaws apart. From this soldier's belt too, on a gold watch-chain, there hung a pair of pincers.

According to the signpost, Abda was still three kilometres away, yet Walter could hear church bells ringing noon. Heavy anti-aircraft batteries guarded the supply corps base, a big farmyard with buildings on all four sides, and Walter took his bike to the vehicle repair supervisor and hung up his luggage in the driver's room beside the stables. The command office on the ground floor of the house — practically a castle — was filled with the clatter of typewriters, and the visibly exhausted Troche, the Hauptsturmführer's adjutant, examined Walter's marching orders. 'Well, look at this!' he said. 'People are even coming back . . . Nice trip? Good weather?' He put a cigarette in his mouth and walked to the telephone. 'Eat and stay prepared!'

Walter closed the door, following the signs. In a room full of paintings and mirrors lay wounded men, most of them on straw, and as for the kitchen, nothing had been cooked there in quite some time: doctors and orderlies in dirty coats were standing around the work table; arms and legs red and blue with gangrene were sticking out of the sink. A nurse shook her head and pointed to the open barn at the back of the farmyard. In the storeroom, which held new engines and tank turrets, and whose walls were stacked with cages full of messenger pigeons, there was a mobile field kitchen.

It had a drawbar, and an unharnessed horse dozed beside a hayrack in the corner. Walter filled a tin plate and joined the drivers who were sitting and playing cards at the end of a long table. 'Ah, look who it is!' said Jörn. 'Now we're all here. Did you take your picture?' And when Walter said no and handed him the camera: 'But you've taken a few pictures of Wallachian sheep for me?'

Jörn had been a veterinary student in Hanover, as Walter recalled. He nodded in reply and ate a spoonful of potato soup. The three other men at the table, who were drinking wine from crystal glasses, wore no collar patches; Jörn introduced them to him: Friedhelm and Hermann, school students from Munich, and their bunkmate Florian, an apprentice tanner from Tulln on the Danube. Even though they were similar in age, Florian called the other two 'little lads'; all of them wore new caps, and the

131

light-blue pennants of the supply unit on their sleeves were still clean. Already inebriated, though it was only midday, they argued about the rules of whatever game they were playing and banged the cards down so that the matches they were playing for leaped into the air.

Jörn wasn't sober either. He slid closer to Walter, plucked a hair from his soup and said, 'They don't just infuriate everyone with their farting, they also play like Cossacks — I haven't a chance. August caught it, by the way, August Klander. Our geologist wanted to pick up a shiny stone, but unfortunately there was a mine underneath. Now he'll never have to wash his hands again. Fiete's here, did you know?'

Walter lowered the spoon which was already at his mouth, and nodded towards the road. 'You mean out in Gyõr, in the field hospital?'

Jörn ran his tongue over his teeth and closed his eyes for a moment. 'He's right here,' he said. 'Here in the basement, under lock and key. The stupid bastard . . . '

'But why?' Walter asked. 'How's that possible? He's wounded.'

The clouds drifted apart, and harsh light fell through the barn door and made the tiny pockmarks on Jörn's forehead seem to disappear . . . but his expression remained dark and still; not an eyelid twitched as he answered Walter's question with a silence that was more piercing than any words. It was only after Jörn had taken a sip from his glass that he repeated quietly: 'That stupid bastard. So soon before the end . . . The Yanks are already at the Rhine!'

132

Walter, who had started sweating and was finding it hard to breathe, opened the collar of his jacket. He stared at the horse, an old beast with a bony rump and sagging withers, as Jörn slid his glass over to him and returned to the game, picking up a new hand and looking it over. 'At first I thought I hadn't heard right,' he murmured. 'But there was no mistake. Now, of course, it's looking grim. No one can help him now.'

Walter set his spoon aside, and Friedhelm, a thin boy in a uniform that was too big for him, peered out from under his eyebrows. The red-wine rim on his lip looked like old blood. 'And just guess,' he asked, 'who's going to be throwing him his farewell party?' Swaying on his chair, he drew a card from his hand and pointed around the table with it. 'All of us, our bunk. Which means you too. He's for it, tomorrow morning.'

Friedhelm threw an ace on the table, the others responded, and Walter tipped the remainder of his potato soup in front of the horse. The animal's belly and legs were encrusted with mud, its mane was matted, but where yoke and traces had been its coat was as silkily brown as a yearling's in the sun. Finally, Walter laughed — a dry sound that scratched his throat — before climbing over the bench and saying, 'That's enough, you idiots! You're all drunk! I almost believed your nonsense!' He looked at Jörn. 'It's April Fools' Day, right?'

The horse stamped, and the muddy ground sounded hollow. The senior soldier who was nominally in charge of the bunk didn't reply, or only with a sad smile. He added a few matches to the pot, asked whose turn it was and played a new card that clearly wasn't going to get him anywhere — the schoolboys groaned anyway. The apprentice tanner, a laughing, tow-headed boy, his hands dyed blue, clawed in his gains and said languidly, in an Austrian accent: 'Today's the twentieth of March. Pull yourself together. What are we supposed to do? Orders are orders. If we refuse, it's us against the wall. I'm not going to die for some dreamer. I've got a girl at home!'

★   ★   ★

In the air, the barking of guns. A snub-nosed transport glider made its way towards the field as smoke rose from the hedge. Behind the thumb-smudged panes of glass, one could see the pale faces of Hitler Youth, who clearly weren't flying for the first time. It stayed calmly on course, the runners soon touching the earth, but the Ilyushin that had fired on the glider came back in spite of the ack-ack guns and fired again. Now it caught the rudder and shredded a plywood wing, whereupon the body of the glider tipped sideways and the payload, after a ghostly moment of silence — one boy tried to push it out of a side hatch — exploded, sending flames high in the air.

The blast shattered the windows in the farm, and while his comrades ran across the field with blankets, shovels and buckets, Walter walked

134

under the arcades and down the steps to the basement. His heels echoed louder with each step.

There was only a faint light in the corridor of rusty metal doors. The Sturmmann on a stool beside the radiator was cutting an apple with his bayonet, and when Walter presented his request he shook his head and said, 'You can forget that one, private, at least without a permit. The people behind these doors aren't anybody's friends.' Then he raised his head and studied Walter coldly. 'But if you have tender feelings for a deserter, perhaps we should go and see the boss or something? About sodomy and so on?'

A quiet ringing above their heads. Fine dust fell from the grey wings of a moth fluttering around the lamp; the guard fixed the bayonet back on his rifle. 'You know what we did with the partisans in the mountains, that Tito crowd? Lined them up back to chest and betted on how many would fall over if we shot the first one in the heart or the neck. It's a way of saving ammunition, you can make a few marks and have some fun at the same time. That's how we should deal with our own bastards here. Now, bugger off!'

He spat out some peel and Walter climbed the stairs and paused behind the stacks of tyres and sacks of oats before leaving the farm by a side door. The sky was deep grey now, and wind rustled in the spring grain. With the heat of the burning glider on the back of his neck, he looked through the basement windows along the edge of the field, a long row, all barred. The gaps

135

between the steel strips looked like thorns.

In one of the deep rooms, lit by the glow of flame, where yellowish green and violet turnips were stacked in boxes, two soldiers sat on the stone floor. They weren't wearing boots, just foot wraps, and they kept their heads lowered when Walter's shadow fell over them. Shining on their collars were the embroidered sabres of the Handschar Division — Bosnian Muslims. Their fezzes, which bore the SS death's head, lay on the floor beside them; Walter whistled through his teeth.

A bearded man with thickly swollen eyelids looked up. His fingernails were black and jagged, his knuckles bruised, and when Walter asked him quietly about Fiete, the man shook his head and murmured something incomprehensible. As soon as Walter knelt on the ground, however, pressing his forehead against the bars to look deeper into the room, there was a cough from the cell's darkest corner, a clattering as if of wooden shoes, and suddenly his friend stood under the window, tilting his head back and asking, 'Is that you?'

Judging by his voice, Fiete had a bad cold. Instead of a uniform he was wearing a peasant shirt — once white, now bloodstained — with knots for buttons, as well as a sheep-skin waistcoat and blue canvas trousers. His face looked even more emaciated than it had done days before, and his angular cheekbones stood out; there was a feverish gleam in his eyes. But his arm was no longer in a sling.

'Christ alive, what's wrong with you?' Walter

136

hissed, looking round. A guard had come out of the gate to watch the firefighting work. 'Have you lost your mind? Why didn't you stay in the field hospital?'

But Fiete dismissed this notion with a wave and coughed again, reaching into his shirt and putting a hand on his collarbone through the dirty bandage. He spat out some pus and slumped on a chopping block, and when he crossed his legs a clog slipped from his foot. 'Why, why, what . . . Aren't you full of questions! I just didn't want to go to the front, simple as that.'

Sweat ran down Walter's temples, though he felt as though his blood had turned to ice. He crushed a few nits between his fingernails, hands trembling.

'They'd already put a transport together,' said Fiete. 'Everyone capable of crawling had to go out and fight again, at the front line, and I knew it would be my turn, this time . . . You don't get away with a splinter twice. I don't suppose you've got a smoke, Ata?'

Walter said no with a blink, and Fiete hunched his shoulders and folded his arms in front of his chest. 'Pole Star always over your right ear, that's how you find your way west, I read somewhere. And when it got dark, I went out the window. But there were no stars that night, it was all cloudy, and I trudged for hours through the pitch-dark wilderness — kept ending up in the mud. Until I saw something shimmering in front of me, two silver moons. And you know what one of the cops said to the other?' Drawing in air

137

through his teeth, he scratched in his trouser pocket. ''Look, another romantic.''

Fiete met Walter's stare, and for a moment his eyes lit up. 'By the way . . . Ortrud actually applied for our long-distance wedding, imagine that. At the register office in Schleswig. Who knows, maybe we're married already. I'd rather have had it in Hamburg, but it doesn't matter, I'm not there anyway.' He smiled flatly and winked at Walter. 'She's pregnant, too.'

The black smoke of the fire wafted over. Walter shivered again, his teeth chattering as he let go of the bar over the window. It was raining now, and wet rust stuck to his hands. 'Right then, listen, we've got to do something. I'll have a word with the Hauptsturmführer,' he said and got to his feet. 'I'll go there right now. You weren't in your right mind, and that's all there is to it. Veronal, Pervitin or alcohol. Or all three, because of the pain. They won't just put you up against the wall. You can't shoot down a wounded man, there must be laws . . . I mean, we're soldiers, we've got honour, that's what they're always telling us, isn't it? It's on our belt buckles.'

He looked round again. The guard was taking a swig from his canteen. Walter quickly wriggled out of his coat and stuck it through the bars. 'Hang on to that, it's getting cold. I'll get you some blankets too.'

Fiete stood up to take the coat. 'Thanks,' he croaked and felt the fabric, the fulled wool, specially manufactured for drivers; the inside lining rarely got wet. 'I could use a bit of sulphur ointment, for the itching. But tobacco more than anything!' Then he wrapped himself in the coat, slumped back on the block and murmured, 'Well, what's the point? I'd never have known which star was the right one anyway.'

Walter nodded to him. The gutters dripped above. Curtains blew from the broken windows of the building. The transport glider was almost extinguished. A few soldiers shovelled soil onto the remaining embers, others dragged away boxes of rescued cargo, probably rifles, while the corpses of the two Hitler Youth lay, charred and smoking, on the spring grain. Crows squatted in the trees.

★ ★ ★

The ashtrays under the table lamps were full to overflowing, and when the clatter of the typewriters paused for a moment you could hear the quick footsteps of the nurses and the wounded in the mirrored hall. The Hauptsturm-führer's adjutant pulled a couple of green flags from the map on the wall to move them a bit further west, meanwhile taking stock of Walter out of the corner of his eye: 'Why aren't you standing to attention, private? What's up?'

Walter straightened his back. He nodded towards the bright stained glass of the commander's broad office door; the handle was an ivory fish that looked as if its scales were made of dirty fingernails. 'I would like to speak to Herr Hauptsturmführer Greiff, please. On a personal matter.'

'Oho!' said Troche, himself an Unterscharfü-
hrer, a gaunt man with a scarred face. 'A
personal matter . . . That does sound very
exciting. What might it be this time? A trip
around the Alps? A seaside holiday by the
Adriatic?' He whipped open the duty book to
its last few pages, crossed something out and
said, 'You're having far too nice a time of it,
young man! Now, ride like lightning to Gyõr and
get the rest of the medicine from the field
hospital, and bring back a receipt. I want to
see you in two hours, dead or alive. Get out of
here!'

He spat a chewed match on the floor and
turned the telephone crank, but Walter stayed
where he was. Eyes lowered, he clasped his
hands behind his back and persisted: 'Please, I'd
like to talk to the Hauptsturmführer. It's urgent.
I helped his son, and he assured me I could
approach him any time. It's about a comrade this
time, not about me!'

But the officer gestured to Walter to be quiet.
He moved two red flags and put through a few
coordinates, speaking loudly to overcome the
sounds of shooting, wailing and crashing that
rang out of the receiver. His secretary, with
sleeve guards over his uniform, raised his head
and pointed to the text he was in the middle of
typing. 'Old Greiff went up in smoke yesterday,'
he said. 'Along with the last bridge. You might
find something on the shore, I suppose — a heel
or maybe even an ear you could whisper your
problems into . . .'

He contorted his mouth into a bilious grin,

140

and Walter turned round and looked into the hospital room where a nurse was kneeling on the floor taking the bandages off a dead man to use them again straight away on a living one. Walter hesitated, stared for a moment at the tips of his boots, the jagged soles to which soil was still clinging, and at last he took a deep breath, reached for the ivory handle and found himself — he knocked and walked in simultaneously — in the commander's room.

It was a drawing room with burgundy fabric wallpaper and pale frescoes on the ceiling, and the two-tone block parquet made it look bigger than it was. In it were a kind of sofa with only one armrest, a big old globe, shelves full of rolled-up maps and files, and a desk. The inside shutters, painted with garlands, were closed, and the officer sitting in the lamplight didn't look up. He just flicked the pages of a book and said, 'Finished already?'

He wore braided shoulder boards, his collar patch was framed in silver and one of the four stars it bore had a brand-new sheen: a Sturmbannführer, a fat man with fair hair and horn-rimmed glasses. He didn't look up until Walter clicked his heels together and saluted. His wide lips were slack, his mouth bored. 'Well now!' he said. 'Who let you in?' According to the sign on the desk his name was Domberg, and his ill-shaven double chin wobbled along when he shook his head. 'Are you in my company? Or do you want to shoot me?'

His voice sounded strangely thin and defensive; but in fact it was that of a man who was

141

used to having his quiet observations listened to, and Walter couldn't help smiling. 'Shoot you? Why? I'm not even carrying a gun.' But then he cleared his throat, gave his name, rank and serial number and said, 'I've come for a comrade. He's in the basement with the turnips.'

Domberg nodded and went on flicking through the pages of the book, a big leather Bible full of hand-painted initials and golden haloes, as the groans of the wounded came through the door. 'About, not for,' he said, reaching into the drawer and lighting a cigarette. 'You have come *about* a comrade. How much schooling do you have?'

He put his Triplex lighter down in front of him, and Walter, who forgot for a moment to stand to attention, shrugged his shoulders. 'Who do you mean, me? Well, normal,' he replied. 'Horst Wessel elementary school, Essen-Borbeck. I've come about Fiete Caroli, Sturmbannführer. Friedrich Caroli, I mean. He's to be executed tomorrow, and I would like most respectfully to ask you to — '

The officer raised his hand. The pale blue smoke drifting over the table smelled for a moment like perfume, sweet and sharp. 'Elementary school may be normal,' he said. 'And I know many consider it sufficient . . . But it's not enough, young man. Listen to yourself: *most respectively!* What a mangling of the German language. One is respectful — that word, particularly for a soldier, contains all levels of meaning — or else one is not. One may be more *alive* than one's fellow man, but no one who has

142

been shot is more dead than another . . . do you understand?'

Walter nodded hesitantly and said, 'Yes. I'm sorry. I would just like to ask — '

'No!' the officer shouted, and unscrewed the lid of a dented metal thermos. 'Stick to the subject, if you would be so kind, private! How can you be in my troop if you have difficulties with elementary grammar? Now: *about*, in the German language, takes the genitive case. What is the genitive? Or is it genius? Or *genital*?' Lips pursed, he stuck out his chin; his eyes were grey, with dark pupils. 'So? I'm waiting for an answer.'

Walter, who was feeling hot, had to swallow. 'Well, it's a case,' he said and ran his hand over the back of his neck. 'The genitive case, the second one. First there's the nominative case and after that the accusative and the dative.'

Domberg poured coffee into a cup with painted roses — real bean coffee, apparently — and put in a spoonful of sugar. 'So, Germany isn't quite lost after all. And what do you think is the point of that genitive case? Of what use might it be?'

He stirred his coffee, studying Walter, and drew once more on his cigarette, letting the smoke out very slowly through his nose. The crystal droplets on the edge of his lampshade trembled slightly every time a tank or a bulldozer crossed the farmyard. 'It's no use at all!' Domberg said and grinned. 'The language manages perfectly well without it. Because if you write 'the cowardice of my friend' or 'my friend's cowardice' it makes not a whit of difference, does it? We both know what it means.'

He raised a finger and arched his brows. 'And yet, and yet . . . It does something to us, that genitive does. It changes our attitude. History's prisms, the day's last glow — can you hear that? That quiet bronze tone?' He arched his finger. 'It refines our souls, young man, and teaches us the meaning of intellectual nobility. The principle of leaving nothing to chance and not always taking the easiest path — that is the genitive! Do you see that?'

Walter nodded, and the officer bent over the table and flicked through the notebook that lay beside his cap. 'So, what was your comrade called? Caroli? Friedrich Caroli? A lovely name, isn't it? One for whom peace — Frieden — is enough. He was the north German with the poetry in his pocket, I remember.' Eyes narrowed, he looked up to the ceiling and moved his lips mutely for a moment. Then he raised one arm and waved his hand through the smoke, declaiming, 'God has leisure. / Others were left to do a hard day's work / My fate to rest beneath the feet / of the grieving, loquacious winds // And if the ancient grape / the black grape, returning dusty and warm / always revives my faith / Sigh no more, God will not grow poor.'

Domberg smiled crookedly, revealing a canine. 'That Loerke isn't bad, your comrade has good taste. But in the end, what can we do? He has executed himself. It's out of my hands now, I fear. Nothing I can do.' Coughing, he closed the notebook, stubbed out his half-smoked cigarette and folded his fingers over his belly. 'Our Führer

144

put it well: a soldier *can* die, but a deserter *must* die. Request a visitor's pass and go see him, young man. He'll soon know more than the rest of us.'

He pointed to the door, took a drink and flicked again through the pages of the illustrated volume. Their gold edges flashed like blades. But Walter didn't move, and when Domberg blew a gauzy sheet of protective paper off a picture of the Madonna and asked in a strangely muted voice, as if he hadn't opened his mouth, what else Walter wanted, he even stepped towards the table, took off his cap and said, 'Please, Sturmbannführer — Fiete didn't want to desert, I'm sure of it. I know him, we used to live under the same roof and work together, up at the Kaiser Wilhelm Canal. He's a clown, he doesn't think three steps ahead, and when he first joined us at the farm he didn't know a rake from a pitchfork. But the animals liked him, the calves licked his hands, and that's got to mean something. I mean, he's a great fellow, a brave soldier, he always had energy during basic training, and he shot more accurately than lots of people — more than me, even! He's delicate, but he isn't a coward, on the contrary — he's never shied away from dirty work . . . '

The officer struggled to hide a yawn; his chin crinkled, and he folded his arms and crossed his legs. The black tips of his boots flashed from under the table. 'What work exactly? What did you do?'

Walter gulped. 'We . . . We're milkers. Or at least I am, I recently took my apprentice exam.

145

Fiete's just starting out. He was at grammar school before. We worked at Major General van Cleef's farm near Sehestedt, and we've — '

'Milkers?' the officer interrupted. 'What a fine and honourable job. In fact, I come from the country myself, near Königsberg. Three hundred hectares. Mostly wheat, but also milk cattle. Our milkers were always innocent fellows, tanned, with marvellous biceps. You could have dropped a knife on them, point first, and it would have bounced. The girls in the hay had fun with them too, with all that junket they ate.' Chuckling, he rubbed his chin. 'But let's not mince words: will people still need milkers in future? Isn't it yesterday's work? Soon it'll be done by machine, don't you think?'

He leaned to the side and ate a spoonful of sugar direct from the pot — a quick, greedy movement — and relieved by his cordial tone Walter shook his head. 'No, that's not going to happen, Sturmbannführer. I don't think so. You learn for three years solid, and to get an udder properly empty you need not just strength but sensitive fingertips. Otherwise you leave remnants in the teats, and everything gets inflamed. Every cow wants to be milked differently, and if you do it wrong she kicks the bucket over. And there are other things you have to do: bring the bull to the heifer and take care that he doesn't break her back, help with the birth and recognize and treat illnesses. Or carry out emergency slaughters or cut dead calves from their mothers. And there are no machines to do that.'

The officer curled one corner of his mouth,

146

which still had a few sugar crystals stuck to it: it almost looked like a smile. Light caught in the pale tortoiseshell frame of his glasses and gave them a reddish rim, but when he took them off his eyes suddenly looked much closer together, and as he stared coldly, fine wrinkles swarmed beneath them. Walter regained his composure, took a breath and said, 'Fiete, I mean Friedrich Caroli, is wounded, Sturmbannführer. He got a splinter and suffered from very severe pain that didn't let him sleep, and people do stupid things when that happens . . . He'd probably taken all kinds of tablets, and mixed them with alcohol. I'm sure he did that, in fact — he has no sense of moderation. His brain was fogged and he just wanted to get some fresh air, I think. And suddenly the Feldjägerkorps were standing in front of him.'

The other man clicked his tongue quietly and poured himself another cup of coffee, as Walter lowered his head and continued: 'He's just turned eighteen, Sturmbannführer. His parents were burned to death in Hamburg, in the air raids, and his girlfriend has applied for a long-distance wedding. She's pregnant . . . I know her, she's a really fine and respectable girl, Ortrud, she'll whip him into shape . . . Please, don't have him shot!' He closed his eyes for a moment, twisted his cap and added more quietly, 'I'll take his place if you like. You can send me to the front, to wherever he was going to be deployed. He can drive a tractor, so he'll be able to deal with a Krupp or a Borgward, and you wouldn't be short-handed here . . . He's my

147

friend, Herr Domberg, I mean Sturmbannführer, a really valuable human being. He'll put
everything right.'

Steam rose from the open thermos, and the
officer stared at the picture in his book, the
Madonna in her blue robe, reading in a field of
flowers. When he drank, a drop of coffee ran
down the cup, but then hung from its underside.
'Your friend, your dear friend . . . ' He shook his
head; his nostrils twitched. 'How long do you
think I need to go on hearing that, private?
Come to your senses! You're speaking up in all
seriousness for a boy who wanted to leave you
and your comrades in the lurch? Who doesn't
care whether the Russians invade our homeland,
kill our best men, dishonour our women and
tread German culture into the mud? A traitor to
the Fatherland? You're standing here defending
cowardice and telling me seriously that this
criminal was a good man because your calves
licked his hands?'

The drop of coffee fell on the book that the
Madonna was holding in her lap, although Domberg
didn't notice. Walter wanted to say something,
but the officer raised his chin and put his glasses
back on; when he spoke, his voice had taken on a
glassy edge: 'Listen to me, Urban! Apart from
the fact that I could cashier you for your partisan-
ship on this boy's behalf: in war it is not about
what someone wants, feels or thinks, in war the
only thing that matters is how someone acts
— you must know that, no? And this man, who
wears on his belt buckle — as we all do — the
words *My honour is loyalty*, has done the worst

148

thing a soldier can do — he wasn't even cowardly in the face of the enemy! Oh, no! That would be understandable, under certain circumstances. Instead . . . Well, if a bullet catches you tomorrow, it's probably because unprincipled boys like him have thrown in the towel.' He looked at the cap in Walter's hand. 'And now put on your cap and close the door behind you! My patience has limits! You and your bunkmates will shoot your friend tomorrow morning, as you've been ordered to do, and if you refuse, or get it into your heads to play sick, you can go to the wall too. Is that clear?'

Domberg waved Walter out, a movement from the wrist that bumped against the rocker blotter beside his lamp. The shadow of its handle, a small bronze eagle, slid enlarged across the wallpaper, and without being aware of it, Walter took another step forwards, to the desk. His eyes were moist, stinging, and his pulse thumped so hard in his ears that he himself could barely hear what he was saying between clenched teeth. But Domberg, who had turned the page of his book, only shrugged. ' ''Why, why . . . ?'' His voice was soft and defensive again now, and he lit a new cigarette and sighed as he exhaled the smoke. 'Out of humanity, of course. Because you're his friend, as you say. You'll take good aim so that he doesn't suffer.'

★ ★ ★

The bell in the village church was ringing for evening Mass when Walter came back from

Győr. It was still raining, and after he had unloaded the medical supplies he picked up a breadbag and ran to the basement. Blood on the steps, the outline of a boot in a dried pool, brownish scrapes on the plaster. The guard, a different one, was cleaning his teeth with a wood chip. He gave a start when Walter handed him his handwritten visitor's permit. 'It's even got a stamp on it,' the guard said as he opened the metal door. 'How elegantly the world ends!'

The turnips smelled sweetly earthy, and Fiete's coat buttons shone in the beam of light that fell into the darkness. One of the two fezzes lay crushed on the floor; Fiete got slowly up from his bed, a pile of straw. He clung to the wall and knocked over a bowl; the guard closed the door again and said, already half behind the metal barrier, 'Keep it brief, comrades. It says ten minutes on the chit.'

The lock snapped shut, and in the sudden silence the sound of rain grew louder. The last of the daylight shone above the field, and without saying a word Walter unclipped the rolled-up blanket from his belt and threw it on the straw. Then he took a candle from his breadbag, lit it and opened the brandy that he had bought from the quartermaster, an Italian brand. His hand was trembling and the screw top clicked quietly against the glass as he avoided his friend's eye, the frightened question in it. Walter looked up mutely at the bars with their twisted thorns. A draught stirred the dusty cobwebs under the blanket.

Fiete, whose chest sank, shut his eyes for a

moment. He grasped the bottle with both hands and took a sip. They sat down on the straw and Walter took a bar of chocolate, a corner of bread, some dried sausage and two packs of cigarettes from the breadbag, a special tobacco mixture. He had also managed to drum up some sulphur ointment, and while he squeezed some from the tube he looked round; there was no one else in the room, the extent of which one could only guess at in the sparse light. The shadows of the piles of turnips reached almost to the brick vault, where moss and grass hung from the cracks.

'Where are the two Bosnians?' Walter asked quietly, but Fiete, with the bottle between his knees, only gestured vaguely. Walter asked him to lower his head and rubbed the ointment on the scratches amid the stubble. Then Walter unbuttoned Fiete's coat and shirt, lifted his healthy arm and checked his armpit. Countless nits were stuck among the sweaty hairs, smaller than sesame seeds, a feeling like sand under his fingertips; he took his comb from his pocket, raked the nits out as best he could, and rubbed some ointment there as well. It burned under his fingernails.

Guns sounded through the rain, light artillery beyond the Raab. Again and again the noise was drowned by the wind, and Fiete now drank in longer draughts, the brandy spilling from the corner of his mouth and dripping onto his collarbone and the encrusted bandage. But when Walter suggested putting on a new one — he had brought bandages with him — Fiete didn't even shake his head. He just looked at Walter silently,

151

askance, apparently full of bitter amusement, and tapped a cigarette out of the pack.

Cheap tobacco crackled over the candle flame, and Fiete's first drag was followed by a fit of coughing, after which he spat out mucus and a little blood. Eyes gleaming, he stared at the candle on the floor, its little white flame, beneath which the candle wax melted like water. 'Well,' he said thickly and took another drag, 'I tried.' He licked his cracked lips and repeated the words, louder, as if against the rain and the gunfire outside. 'At least I tried, damn it! And that's what counts, isn't it?'

Something seemed to be bubbling in Fiete's bronchia and Walter nodded hesitantly. A shape moved in the darkness, and Walter narrowed his eyes to see more clearly. A rat scuttled over the rim of a supply case, a black creature with a lighter tail; it retreated among the turnips when Walter threw a lump of plaster. He saw there were tooth marks gnawed into the sweet centres of the vegetables. He cracked a few nits that were still stuck to his fingers and said, 'Who knows . . . Perhaps the Russians will be here sooner than we think. Maybe even tomorrow morning.'

The wax flowed onto the stone floor, and Fiete, frowning, shook his head. 'That wouldn't help — they don't distinguish between volunteers and forced recruits, Ata. They shoot every SS man on sight, haven't you heard?'

Drinking, Fiete stared at his clogs. The wood was cracked and lined with leather at the ankles, and he pressed the tips together and groaned, 'Christ, what am I doing here. I mean, if I'd voted for Hitler, like most of them ... But I wanted nothing to do with this mess, any more than you did. I have no enemies, at least none that want to kill me. This is a war for cynics, who don't believe in anything but might makes right ... when in fact they're only mediocrities and weaklings, I found that out in the field. Kick downwards, bow and scrape upwards, and massacre women and children.' With his cigarette in his mouth he squeezed some ointment onto his fingers and said more quietly, as if to himself, 'And those are the men who'll be allowed to blow out my light.'

He put his hand into the waist of his trousers and rubbed his pubic region; both Fiete and Walter gave a start when a door banged nearby. Voices could be heard, drunken laughter, a dog barking. ' 'Milli', her name is,' someone called, 'Melitta in fact. She'll throw the bone saw at your head!' With his lips almost white, Fiete closed his eyes and sank against the worn plaster of the wall. A moment later the men went away; the corridor was quiet again apart from the footsteps of the guard, who whistled sometimes to drive away the boredom. Every few heartbeats the chink in the doorway darkened.

Fiete gulped. 'The strange thing is that I've often dreamed of being shot,' he said. 'Over the last few years I've been shot again and again, and sometimes it was even an act of kindness, of deliverance. For example, if I'd lost my will to live, or was heartbroken, or world-weary or whatever ... Peace at last, I thought — you — can all fuck off, you idiots. But mostly I sat up

153

straight in bed with my hands on my chest and could hardly breathe.'

The cigarette had gone out and Fiete held it to the flame again. 'My father was a doctor, a medical researcher and orderly, did I ever tell you that? In the last war, long before I was born, he was injured several times — snipers. He had a bad limp. And later, when he'd been taken prisoner by the French, somewhere on the Rhône, they made him dig his own grave three times. They'd blindfold him, so he thought he was about to be executed. They yelled orders, loaded their carbines — but then the Frogs just pissed in the hole and he had to fill it up again. He was a good fellow . . . he cried a lot when he talked about the war.'

Fiete spat out some tobacco. 'And once, when I mentioned my dreams, he told me that the cells of our bodies have memories, semen and ovaries too, and that's what gets passed down. If you're mentally or physically injured it does something to the next generation. The insults, the blows or the bullets that hit you also injure your own unborn child, so to speak. And later on, however well you bring them up, they're terrified of being insulted, beaten or shot. At least in the subconscious, in their dreams. It makes sense . . . it's logical, don't you think?'

He flicked away what was left of his cigarette and took another drink. A fine spray of water was blowing through the bars now. Walter smoothed some of the cooling, almost solidified candle wax back up around the wick. 'What about the one who has to do the shooting?' he asked

154

tonelessly, after clearing his throat. 'What does he inherit?'

At the edge of the field outside they could see a guard walking past in a hooded coat. A few straws slipped into the wax and caught fire. Fiete scratched the back of his neck. In the glow of the rising flame his face looked for a moment as it had before, like the face of an elegant girl, half covered by the shadow of his arm, and he smiled dully and said, 'How should I know, captain. Probably a great sadness.'

The rain grew quieter. A single chime rang in the village. Fiete handed Walter the bottle, drew up the blanket under his chin and rested his head on his friend's shoulder. Walter sipped at the brandy, which burned his throat and stomach but didn't warm him. Holding his breath, he closed his eyes when he felt his friend's hand touching his cheek, neck and chest quite unselfconsciously, unconcerned about encountering opposition. It was a silent assurance — a final one, in fact, and Walter averted his head to hide his tears.

Fiete coughed again. 'Do you remember that sick dog in Malente, Ata? That stray street dog with the frothing mouth? How it came charging across the playground at training school with bloodshot eyes and everyone shouted and ran away? Christ, he was a brute! He panted as if he'd swallowed something red hot. And suddenly I was the only one standing there, with my back to the wall, and he hobbled over to me like the devil himself. Remember?'

Tracer flares rose into the sky outside, and

Walter nodded. Fiete spat more mucus. 'I was almost fainting with fear. Why me? I wondered at the time. Why me of all people, damn it? Everyone was gawping from behind the window, and I actually saw myself dead or in hospital, and I thought — but it was more of a feeling than a thought — yes, just a moment, why not? Why *not* me? And suddenly I was filled with a freedom, Ata, like I'd never experienced before. I felt very light. I didn't feel fear any more — or, anyway, felt it a lot less — and that beast from hell, that poor dog, actually turned round . . . ' He shook his head and snorted quietly. 'Crazy, isn't it? He'd have finished me off in no time.'

Walter, giving Fiete back the bottle, didn't say anything, couldn't think of anything to say. His friend tipped down what was left of the brandy and threw it into the turnip pile, where it landed intact — there was no crash of breaking glass — though it started some of the vegetables rolling, culminating in a dull thud that sounded like wood or bones, and which was itself followed by a cloud of dust. Greyish brown, the dust billowed through the cellar, the candlelight; the spicy smell of soil came from the field, dried in the sun, the autumn of the harvest, and Fiete pressed himself against Walter again and closed his eyes.

His breathing was heavy and slightly wheezy, and the vein in his neck throbbed quickly; Walter could feel the boy shaking, could feel his fear. He peeled wax from his fingers and listened: not a sound in the corridor. The guns on the other side of the river had fallen silent as well; perhaps they

156

might both have nodded off briefly on the straw. To Walter at least, with the cold wind on his back, the squeaking somewhere underneath the turnips sounded like the hissing and whistling of damp logs in childhood campfires. His friend threw part of the blanket over him. 'You're shivering,' Fiete whispered.

At that moment, the key turned in the lock. The corner of the door scraped on the stone floor and the thin metal, a corner of iron, curved inwards and then regained its shape with a snap.

Fiete sat up, grabbed Walter's wrist to look at the watch. Behind the cone of light stood several soldiers. The Sturmbannführer's adjutant carried in a paraffin lamp on a wire and set it down next to the candle. Then he pulled his gloves off, put them in the pockets of his leather coat and winked at his two subordinates. 'Some might speak of luck,' he said. His rousing voice, used to issuing orders, echoed under the vault. 'You need someone to put in a good word for you, Caroli.'

As if intoxicated by the smell of the turnips, moths fluttered into the room from the corridor. The boys looked at each other, and Troche grinned tartly as he bent down and gave the condemned man a yellow envelope. 'With greetings from the boss. Unusually, you are being given permission to inform your closest relatives. No more than twenty-four lines, readable. No place names, no names of comrades or officers, nothing about martial law. Stick to the lines and don't write in the margin.' He pushed up the peak of his cap and looked inquisitively into Fiete's face. 'Have you got that,

157

young man? Name of the recipient on the other side.'

Fiete's eyebrows twitched, but he didn't say a word. He stared past Troche, eyes goggling, at the wax around the wick, flowing again, and it was only when Troche gestured to Walter to leave the room that he slumped in on himself and took a deep breath. 'No, wait!'

He reached for Walter's arm. His pale face contorted with fear, he clawed his hand into Walter's uniform and stood up with him, one foot slipping from its clog. Walter supported Fiete, helped him back into his shoe, and hung the blanket back around his shoulders. With trembling fingers Walter brushed a piece of straw from the fabric, an ear of wheat like gold seen through tears, nodded to Fiete and drew him carefully to him. He'd never embraced a man before, and Fiete, who seemed incredibly slender in spite of the blanket and the coat, and whose chin was still youthfully smooth, rose on tiptoe and said into Walter's ear: 'Good luck, captain. Thanks for everything. And say hello to Ortrud, all right? Say hello to everybody. It'll all be over tomorrow.'

Then he coughed, fought to suppress any further coughs, and asked hoarsely, almost wheezing, 'Will you be there?'

He was panting now. Gravel crunched under the guards' boots, and Walter held his friend tighter, kissed his temple. Fiete's eyes closed and his cracked lips moved without making a sound, as though his throat was paralysed. As Walter pressed his cold brow against Fiete's, which was

158

drenched with sweat, and ran his hand over the stubble of Fiete's hair, he couldn't even swallow. Fiete groaned through gritted teeth, and Walter patted him gently on the back and repeated: 'It's fine, Imi. They're all idiots. Tomorrow nothing will hurt you any more.'

The wind blew through the bars, the soldiers in the corridor held a whispered conversation, and both Walter and Fiete had stopped crying by the time they parted at last, looking at each other for another few heartbeats. Their eyes darkened, just a little, but enough that their colours, pale blue and greenish brown, could no longer be told apart. Troche stamped out the candle stub with his heel and clapped his hands. 'Right, off we go, we haven't got all night!' he said. 'Write your letter, Caroli!'

Fiete looked round, supporting himself on the wall. Grains of sand trickled from the rotting plaster. 'What do you mean? Now?' Raising his scabby eyebrows, he pulled the blanket up under his chin. 'You want me to write it now?'

'Of course!' said the adjutant and reached into his coat pocket. 'Why do you think I'm hanging around? I'm waiting!'

He took out a fountain pen, unscrewed it and once again ordered Walter to leave the room. Walter nodded to the condemned man, accidentally kicking a discarded belt on the floor that lay beside the fez. The buckle rattled as he stepped backwards, his shadow broadening on the floor and the wall, losing itself in the dark behind the bars. 'So, till tomorrow,' he said hoarsely. 'I'll be there.'

But Fiete didn't look up. He had set the piece of paper down by the paraffin lamp and now wrote kneeling, with his forearms on the floor. The blanket had slipped down to the back of his neck and his head was barely visible. The corners of the blanket covered his hands, and the emblem on the cap of the fountain pen, a kind of snowflake, shimmered dimly. 'Thank you,' he said, and went on writing.

★ ★ ★

The temperature dropped during the night, and in the morning thin ice lay over the puddles. Half sunk in the morass, an anti-aircraft gun stood on the mound beyond the field. The first birds sang and the pale reeds swayed as an old boar walked to the water. A massive beast with bristles that stood on end, dew-drenched, on the back of its neck, it raised its snout and sniffed, then studied the fir trees on the opposite shore with narrow eyes before bending down and browsing on the duckweed. Its ear-tips twitched, its tail twirled contentedly. Then it rolled grunting in the mud, the smell of ammonia filled the air, and after rubbing its steaming hide and sharpening its long tusks against an oak tree — the bark cracked and split, teeth squeaked against the white wood — the lonely bath was soon over, and the boar vanished as quietly as it had come.

Frost lay on the two graves behind the barn — narrow heaps bearing the boot prints of the soldiers who had tramped the earth down the previous day. The men sat at the end of the long

160

table eating jam and bread, and Jörn was pouring tea for them from a big metal jug. He wore fingerless gloves and a field cap with earflaps, and while the apprentice tanner and the schoolboys were fanning their cards, Jörn waved Walter over and held out a cup. 'You look awful. Didn't you get any sleep?'

At first Walter didn't reply, or only with a brief movement of his head, then he joined them. Five cleaned and oiled carbines with walnut stocks and oxidized barrels leaned against the wall with five helmets hanging from their muzzles. Walter wrapped his hands around the hot metal cup and said, 'I tried to see him again . . . but the guards . . . Forget it. Sometimes I could hear him coughing in the hole, and it sounded as though he was already under the ground.'

Jörn looked Walter over carefully, reached his arm across the table and tried to feel his forehead with the backs of his fingers, but Walter flinched away. Jörn poured some schnapps into Walter's tea from his silver hip flask. 'Don't think about it too much,' he said. 'Your darkest hour is just dark and that's that, these days you've just got to chalk that one up to fate. And for the lad, it's probably not as bad as you think. At university, I jumped off the scaffolding once, from the second floor, and I can't remember how I even got up there. I had already lost consciousness before I landed. It's a kind of mercy if you're about to have a hard landing.'

An officer shook the posts at the top of the field, three alder trunks, to check their soundness. A stethoscope dangled from the pocket of his fur jacket.

Jörn rubbed and kneaded his fingers. 'Well, Christ on a bike, there I was thinking spring was on the way! Where's your coat? Aren't you freezing your arse off?'

Walter, eyes closed, drank again. The tea was very sweet, so much so that he could barely taste the schnapps. 'Fiete has it,' he said into the cup, then added quietly, 'I'm going to try and miss anyway . . . '

The schoolboys were biting into their rolls and arguing about the sequence of the game, but Florian, the apprentice tanner, had heard what Walter said. He ran the corner of a card down his Adam's apple and said, 'Don't be an idiot — he's going to die no matter what. They'll count the bullets, and if there's one missing they'll send us all to the front before lunch. This very evening we'll just be guts lying in tank tracks.'

The schoolboys looked up and Jörn folded his arms in front of his chest; he spoke quietly, almost conspiratorially. 'He's right, Walter. Don't drop us all in it! Fiete will go on living in the next world, believe me. In a kind of dream that you don't ever have to wake up from. I bet he won't even recognize us.'

He pointed to the carbines with his thumb. 'And one of them will be a blank anyway. So anyone can imagine . . . '

He didn't finish his sentence, and Walter looked at him. 'How do you know that?' he asked, but didn't get an answer. The horse in the corner turned its head.

162

The Sturmbannführer entered the barn, then, leading a little retinue, his adjutant clicking his fingers. The soldiers climbed over their benches and stood to attention, and Domberg, his glasses dusty, his eyes red in their deep cavities, raised his unshaven chin and studied the row man by man. He even straightened a belt buckle and adjusted a collar. It was only when he came to Walter that he relaxed his gaze. Then he looked at his watch and put his hands in his pockets.

His coat stretched over his belly and his fatty neck wobbled when he barked, 'So, gentlemen, I expect manliness and character. There are situations in war when you have to be stronger than your own scruples. Anyone who gives up on our fateful struggle at this crucial hour gives us all up for lost, and has squandered the right to live in our midst. Let's be clear about this — the man who will shortly stand facing your rifles is not a comrade but an enemy. He has trodden our honour and loyalty underfoot, and for that there can be but one punishment.'

Sirens sounded in Gyõr, an air raid. Domberg straightened his glasses and threatened his troops with a finger. 'By the way: in case any of you were thinking of refusing the order, I must remind you that such a man would receive no sympathy from me.' Though his tone of voice was now quite conversational, it sounded, if anything, more penetrating than before, as if his words were themselves made up of icy air. 'Such a man would know, I hope, where he too would be made to stand.' His tongue slipped along the bottom row of his teeth. 'Is that clear to everyone?'

As one they all said, 'Yes, Sturmbannführer!' and he saluted them limply, giving more of a wave, hardly moving his arm, before nodding to his adjutant and leaving the room. As he did so he clapped the horse in the corner on its dusty neck.

Troche, whose scars were paler that morning, paler even than the rest of his face, took off his cap, put on a steel helmet and gestured to the squad to do the same. In spite of the leather inner linings, the cold metal of the helmets could be felt on their shaven heads, and as they fastened the straps Troche pointed to their weapons and said, 'So, let's sort this thing out. I'm sure everyone knows the rules of the game. You stand shoulder to shoulder, release your safety catches at the same time, aim for the chest, and wait for my order. No one is to look the criminal in the eyes, no one is to address a word to him. So out you go now, take up your positions!'

From high above them came the sound of Russian bombers, a big Tupolev squadron heading towards Vienna, as they did almost every morning. One plane dropped flyers, the *Front News* — even glancing at a copy was to risk punishment — which rained down just as the men stepped out of the barn, just as Fiete was being led into the courtyard by two paratroopers. He was in his stocking feet but still wore Walter's coat, which was plainly too big for him; only his fingers peeped out of the sleeves. A ragged strip of his bandage, stained with old blood, hung from the neck of the coat.

He wasn't handcuffed, and his escort only grabbed for his arms when he stumbled over a frozen molehill. One of them held a pistol and was telling the prisoner something out of the corner of his mouth, to which Fiete responded with a nod. He held himself straight and seemed at first glance to be quite calm; but his breath, visible in the early frost, came in short, quick pants. His little clouds were wispy and negligible compared to those of his guards.

They placed him with his back against the middle alder post. Troche took a rope out of his coat. The hemp whistled along the leather edge of his pocket and he tied Fiete's hands behind the wood, a double knot, then gestured with his boot tips for Fiete to put his feet closer together and nearer to the post, before he tied them too. Then he produced a knife, cut the top metal buttons from Walter's coat, and flapped the lapels back so that Fiete's chest formed a smooth surface.

Fiete allowed him to do all this in silence, his eyes lowered, and shook his head almost imperceptibly when the officer, who had taken out a case, tried to put a cigarette between his lips. Fiete raised his chin and looked at the gunners.

His eyes were feverish, his nose and ears red with cold. He frowned and opened his mouth, but Walter wasn't sure if the kid could see him or not, since the sun was shining into his face. Fiete craned his neck a little, lifting his shoulders, possibly looking for Walter among the men standing around, but, having looked, seemed not to recognize him — as if his hopelessness had turned even his best friend, with the steel rim of his helmet over his eyes, his rifle by his foot, into a stranger. He let his shoulders sink again.

A few other soldiers, clutching bread rolls and mugs of steaming tea, came and stood, curious, in the barn door. As Troche walked the barely ten paces from the post to the riflemen, the legs of his riding boots creaking, he studied each of the executioners very carefully. He lit up the cigarette that Fiete had refused, nodding to them, at which they shouldered their carbines and released the safety catches, a quick movement of the thumb, and while Walter held his finger under the metal button, the click of the other catches rang out in the clear, frosty air. Fiete, whose breathing had grown more violent, closed his eyes and moved his lips very slightly.

'What's up with your coat?' Florian hissed from behind the butt of his rifle. 'Are you really going to let him have it?'

But Walter said nothing, and looked past the tanner's blue-dyed hands at Troche, who was now standing beside their rank, but who didn't turn to face the condemned man. Instead, he reached under the gun barrel of one of the schoolboys, carefully corrected his aim, took a drag on the cigarette, then said quietly, almost in a whisper: 'Everyone ready? And . . . fire!' At which Walter, who had expected a different, louder order, already saw smoke in front of his comrades' guns before finally pulling his own

166

trigger, more a reflex than the execution of an order. The echo rang in his ears.

A bullet that had passed through the body sprayed up soil on the far side of the post. Blackbirds flew from the ploughed field, and faster than his amazement at the force of the impacts could register on his face, Fiete slumped slightly, standing there bow-legged. As children do when they feel an unexpected pain, one that they have never experienced and perhaps would never have considered possible. Fiete opened his mouth wide, but kept his eyes closed. Faint steam escaped from the entry holes. The safety catches clicked on again.

His whole body trembling, Fiete managed to straighten his legs once more, but his torso slowly tilted forward, his frown disappeared, and his sudden pallor was no longer that of a living person. The hemp rope scraped along the tree bark, which had burst here and there; blood gleamed on the pale wood; and laboriously, as if he still couldn't believe it, Fiete shook his head. A clear thread of saliva on his lower lip turned bright red.

Then his chin sank to his chest, and Walter, clutching in his fist the hot barrel of his gun, closed his eyes for a moment. He felt dizzy, his guts grumbled, and he involuntarily gritted his teeth when someone behind them said, 'Good shots!' Pushing the brim of his helmet off his forehead, he wiped the sweat from his face with his sleeve, and then there was his friend lying twisted on the ground, and the officer who had cut him from the post ordered them all to

167

present themselves for driving duty in five minutes.

He wrote something in his notebook. The men leaned their carbines against the wall and went into the barn. But Fiete wasn't dead: his lower lip was trembling, his ribcage moved up and down, one of his hands reached into the air. As the doctor bent over him and moved aside the flap of Walter's coat to count the entry wounds — he tapped them off with his pencil — the boy was still exhaling through his nose and mouth, a delicate, quick-panting breath, and now his eyes slowly opened again, so that his irises were visible: the last flash and the dimming blue of his already directionless gaze.

Throwing his head back, as if to offer them all his throat once more, Fiete seemed to be smiling in that old, reckless way of his, with just one corner of his mouth, and Walter, ignoring Troche's voice, his curt instruction, stumbled across the frozen grass towards his friend, lifting his gun above the ground a little before dropping it again, Walter stopped short. Only his shadow fell upon Fiete, upon his face and his eyes, grey now, while Fiete's last faint breath faded, and his open mouth stayed empty.

A bit of blood on his teeth. The doctor held his stethoscope to the dead man's chest and with the thumb and forefinger of his other hand closed both his eyes. The paratroopers started digging. Their pickaxes and shovels clattered in the cold, and then everything turned pale, as if covered in fog, and Walter felt the molehills and the stones against his back and heard his comrades high above him, their shouts and their hard footsteps, treading the ground firm.

★ ★ ★

Dear Helene! I would like to thank you for your letters and the parcel! Everything got here in time for the party, even though we have changed garrisons several times. At least the mail still seems to be working, and perhaps we will spend next Easter at peace.

I don't know if Mum told you: recently I had a few days' leave and went in search of Dad's grave. He died not far from here, but often the crosses are unmarked, and there are so many . . . You don't know where to start looking. At any rate he lies somewhere in this area, and when the war is over we'll drive over here. There is silence in the Puszta, it's like a room or a vault — as if the dead were pricking their ears.

The biscuits you baked, particularly the chocolate ones, were delicious! Even the dried sausage found a grateful recipient. Incidentally, I'm in the field hospital at the moment, nothing serious. Just my nerves, the orderly says, a kind of shell shock even though I'm still at the base: my face twitches and quivers, there's nothing I can do about it. Shaving now would be dangerous. But that will subside, they're giving me porridge and red wine with honey, as if I was taking a spa cure.

The enemy is advancing rapidly, and we'll be retreating soon, behind the Reich border, where I hope not too many partisans will be lurking. Perhaps we will be deployed near Vienna, and I'll get to see a city at last.

At your age, Easter was still my favourite feast. Because after that everything gets brighter and warmer. I still like it more than Christmas. There are eggs here too, dyed with blue grease, camomile and beetroot, but no birch green — most of the trees have been cut down.

So goodbye, lovely Helene, they're turning out the lights. I hope your cough is better, now that winter is over at last. If you have a damp room, put panes of glass on the floor under the bed, that's what people here do too. And say hello to Mum, if you like. Yours, W.

★　★　★

The last of the fuel had been used up, so all the food they had saved from the depots had to be lugged over the mountains in horse carts and ox carts. Walter led three young donkeys over the pass and was already far ahead of his comrades, who were struggling with the rickety carts and the stubborn draught animals, not least because he gave the beasts sugar from time to time. Nimbler than you'd have thought the bulging sacks on their backs would allow, the donkeys followed Walter across the scree washed down from the slopes by the spring thaw, and didn't bolt the one time the rope slipped out of his hand. They simply stood where they were.

Often tree roots and whole trees had to be cleared from the path; it was midday before the men finally reached a reasonably well-made road, which wound its way down into the valley

170

and towards a little church in a clearing. Then they heard a clear, metallic noise, the ground began vibrating, and small stones trickled down the slope. The animals put their ears back as an olive-green truck with enormous bumpers and barred headlights came round the corner. Armed Americans sat on the flatbed, and the driver, whose face Walter at first assumed had been blackened, stopped right beside him and said over his elbow, 'Hey, man, where are your wheels?'

Grinning, he aimed a pistol at Walter, and even though Walter didn't understand a word, he had to smile as well. As he did so he held his hands just wide enough apart to cover the SS runes on his collar, and looked at his comrades out of the corner of his eye. Some of them were jumping away from their carts and vanishing along the bushy side paths, even though no one was shooting or coming after them. But most of them did as Walter did — came hesitantly closer — and after the food had been unloaded they released their animals into the wild with a clap.

The camp to which the soldiers were brought, after a journey through the night on an open trailer, was in a valley near Wagrain — a good eighty kilometres south of Salzburg, an orderly told Walter. A high barbed-wire fence and steep rocky walls surrounded the area, formerly a meadow: a transit station for a large number of prisoners. The grass was crushed, the ground squelched with every step, their boots were quickly drenched. Latrines had been set up — long boxes made of rough tree trunks — but no

171

cabins, tents or bivouacs for the men; some were already busy digging dips in the earth with empty tin cans or their bare hands to find some protection against the sun and rain.

There was nothing to drink, anywhere, and when the thirst became unbearable Walter lay on his belly like all the others and sucked up puddle water through clenched teeth. Decorations, medals and close-combat clasps shimmered in the mud, and after Walter had passed through the ranks for a while and had a good look around, he too threw away his belt buckle and his perforated dog tag and, borrowing a piece of broken glass from a Wehrmacht soldier, he cut the runes from his jacket.

Walter stood on a hill at the edge of the camp: white mountain tops were visible in the distance, rushes grew from the glittering snow, and a soldier — a corporal — got his attention and pointed out at the countless men. Turned to face the warming sun, many of them had taken off their uniform jackets and shirts and were dozing away, sitting up. Their shaved napes were gaunt, their shoulder blades were angular beneath their dirty undershirts and their arms and hands were scratched and scrawny. 'Take a look,' the corporal said. 'Our thousand-year Reich. What did the Führer say in his New Year's address? He who demands so much from fate is destined for greatness — or something like that. What did he mean, do you think? Diarrhoea and itching?'

The American barracks smelled of cigarette smoke, coffee and fried bacon, but there was nothing for the prisoners to eat, not for two days.

172

Many cooked 'spring soup' in their steel helmets — a broth of young nettles, samphire and dandelion heated by fires fed with their pay books. Walter too crouched beside one of the pots and added his to the flame, and an engineer, a man of around forty, loaned him a spoon. Already grey-haired, the engineer reached into the breast pocket of his shirt and took out some tobacco, and when Walter asked how long they would have to stay there, he shrugged. 'Only for a short time, I think. It's not in the Yanks' interest to keep prisoners. It's too expensive for them.'

He rolled himself a cigarette. The paper had Cyrillic watermarks. 'They're looking for war criminals, SS men. And if you ask me, it serves those bastards right. They always had the newest weapons, the best food and the hottest women, who were always up for it. The Führer and his Himmler blew smoke up their arses and promised them the skies, and still they couldn't save us, not at Balaton and not at Vienna. Let them all rot.'

Walter swallowed: green as spinach, the lukewarm brew smelled very bitter, and sand crunched between his teeth. 'Why war criminals?' he asked. 'How are they going to recognize them?'

The man licked his cigarette paper. 'Well, aren't you a babe in the woods. How will they recognize them? By their tattoos, the blood groups. That's the mark of Cain. And they're checking every single man.'

Walter reached under his shirt and touched

173

the slightly raised spot. A cool breeze ran over the back of his neck. 'But is it — ' he asked, startled — 'is it only the SS who have them? Don't all soldiers have a tattoo like that?'

The engineer's quiet 'Aha!' into the hollow of his hand, as he lit the cigarette, was full of mockery. He blew smoke out of the corner of his mouth and studied the collar of Walter's uniform. 'Not all of them, no. You'll see when you're being deloused . . .'

In the evening it started to rain, and they hung their jackets and coats over their heads. Anyone who still had a tarpaulin or a blanket stretched it with pegs over the hole in the ground where they slept or tried to sleep. But soon everything was full of water, and if the men pressed closer together to find some warmth, the Americans on the other side of the fence fired flares into the darkness. Then sharp-edged shadows grew over the rocky walls, and the burning magnesium dripped from the heights onto the exhausted men, injuring some. Their cries often turned into a loud weeping and whimpering, and when this went on for too long, someone from the barracks would shout, 'Shut up!'

The rain eased off towards morning, the sky cleared, and now some of the men managed to get some sleep in spite of the waterlogged earth; you could even hear the occasional snore. The stars turned pale over the valley, the snowy tips of the mountains assumed a rosy glow, and the wind made the oval dog tags hanging from their chains on the barbed wire, thousands of them, rattle gently against one another.

174

★   ★   ★

Dear Liesel, I hope you are well and in good health. Given the circumstances, I am well. Do not be surprised by the scrawly handwriting. This is special paper that they hand out to us here — when you write on it with water it turns blue, but often it runs and you have to write very carefully.

After a few days near Salzburg in Austria I am now in a former concentration camp near Munich. The Americans are treating us decently. Even when we were being interrogated there was no shouting, and they didn't hit us, or at least not me. Well, I'm young, and I was a forced recruit, and all I did was drive trucks around. We can shower twice a week and can wear their old uniforms, or the uniforms of their dead soldiers. But we have to write POW on the back. I did mine with toothpaste, Colgate. I can wash it out later.

We're waiting and repairing the Americans' cars, otherwise there isn't much to do. Some men climb onto the roofs of the barracks to look into the women's block. Wardresses sit there, real harridans from the Totenkopf-SS. They tied naked prisoners to the fences in the deepest frost and poured water over them, and if they didn't die quickly enough they helped them along with kitchen knives. Now they have nothing to lose and are showing the men what they want to see.

Some men have reading evenings, others put on plays. Sometimes there are even films, and — just imagine — Göring was with us in the cinema yesterday, the Reichsmarschall. There's going to be a big trial in Nuremberg. He came in like Lord Muck,

175

still wearing that big ring, but all the slits for the medals on his jacket were empty. At least twenty military policemen with white helmets and belts sat down around him in such a way that no one could come too close. Then he sat down and watched 'Romance in a Minor Key' with us, and when, at the end, that poor betrayed husband said, 'Finished, finished, it doesn't even hurt any more!' there were tears in his eyes. I saw them glittering.

It's not clear how long we'll have to stay here. Since yesterday they've been saying that young people from the mountains are getting a preferential release so that the economy can get going again, and because I was born in the Ruhr and my family lives there, I may be allowed to leave as a miner. At any rate I'll try — a white lie to be back in the north for the summer. Or do you already have another squeeze? I've often thought of you, and that's how I've stayed well, I fully believe it. One, two, three.

★ ★ ★

The domes of the towers of the Frauenkirche looked almost as they did in postcards or photographs, but in the ruins of the apse lay shattered pews and a crucifix that was missing a Jesus; only his nailed hands still hung from the beam. The paths between the piles of wood and brick were narrow, the dust tasted like chalk on the lips, and Walter joined the crowd waiting by a fire hydrant. They were all carrying buckets, jugs or empty beer pitchers with porcelain caps, and talked to one another in their dialect, of which he understood only a few words, if anything. Two girls, wearing sandals made of car tyres along with their traditional dresses, sharing a cigarette away from the queue, smiled at him.

The heat was oppressive. The pecking sound of the hammers with which the old mortar was being knocked from the bricks came from all directions, and Walter's throat was so dry that he could hardly swallow. He kept trying to clear it. Many of the people in the line laid little boards or bundles of straw on the water so that it didn't splash out of the buckets on their way through the ruins. He nodded to the guard when it was his turn, and held his hands under the tap. But the man looked first at the thirsty man and then at the girls and said, in German, 'Have you got a cup?' and then in English, 'You need a cup.'

The guard wore a dirty neckerchief and his mouth was just a slash in all his stubble. There was no collar on his uniform jacket, but it must have once have belonged to a senior rank; the fabric was officer quality. Where the stripes on the sleeve and the name of his division had been, a spiky wreath gleamed in the sunlight, made up of the ends of faded gold threads. Walter said hoarsely, 'I'm a German. Give me water, comrade.'

With both fists on the handle of the hydrant key, the man studied Walter's mustard-coloured trousers, his short zip-up bomber jacket. 'How am I supposed to do that if you haven't got a cup?' he asked. 'And why are you wearing that Yank gear? Do you work for them?'

'No,' said Walter, 'I was in the camp, the prisoner-of-war camp, and they gave us their clothes. The German uniforms were rotting right off our bones. Now give me water, please. I've been walking for hours.'

The other man gave a start. He had styes in his eyes. 'You've come from the camp? From Dachau? Isn't that where the bigwigs go? What did they give you to eat?'

Walter licked his raw lips. 'To eat? My God, pineapple. Tinned pineapple, every day. Sometimes biscuits. I can't remember what potatoes taste like, let alone meat.' Again, he bent down to the standpipe and held his hands under the opening. 'Come on, I've got to get to the station!'

But the man didn't move. 'Tinned pineapple?' he asked. 'Every day? What luxury. And we have to go into the fields and chew daisies. Look, I'm not giving you any water, not without a cup.'

Walter raised his eyebrows. 'Enough! Where am I supposed to get one of those? Let it run, for heaven's sake! Can't you see that everyone's waiting?'

'Not my problem. Drinking water is precious, you must know that if you've come from the camp. Drinking water can only be dispensed into containers, so that nothing is lost. I have my instructions.'

Walter shook his head in disbelief. He clenched his fists, stepped over the patch of mud in front of the hydrant and asked through his teeth, 'And, excuse me, who gives you those? Your Führer? He's dead, in case you haven't heard!'

He stood with one foot on the tip of the man's

178

shoe; the man lowered his chin and narrowed his eyes. His breath was bad. 'Hello, what's this? Are you threatening me, you filthy Yank? And getting violent while you're about it? You can kiss my arse!'

There was grumbling and cursing when he pulled his rectangular spanner from the hydrant and pushed it behind his belt. With his pelvis jutting and his arms folded, he raised his chin and shouted, 'Listen to this — official announcement: the supply of drinking water is being interrupted until further notice because of infringement of public order. As water guard, I have the right to do this. Objections should be delivered in writing to the city administration. The nearest alternative supply station is at the Stachus.' He gave a nod. 'You can thank this fellow . . .'

Then he climbed over a pile of bricks and disappeared into the basement of a house, of which nothing remained but its firewalls. Crows flew through the nave of the church on the other side of the square, and Walter, whose shirt was sticking to his back, looked around. A few ragged men stepped from the queue and came towards him in silence, including an old man in knee-length lederhosen who set his bucket down in the dust. The expression under his white eyebrows was one of sheer fury.

'What a fool, what an idiot!' he said. 'What a wretch! These are the imbeciles . . . ' He pushed Walter gently aside and turned round. 'What have we got, Huberle? An English one or a French one?'

The man he had addressed, he too in short trousers, with gouty fingers, reached into his rucksack. 'How should I know? Just a spanner.' He took out a brand-new adjustable wrench and tapped it against the hydrant. 'Look, this is aluminium. Like iron, you can whack someone over the head with it, but it's aluminium, you understand? As modern as it gets. So, which way does it go, left or right?'

He licked the tips of his moustache and applied the tool, pressing a foot against the hydrant, and after a quiet gurgling in the pipe, giving off a smell of warm rubber, the water shot across the cobbles in a high arc. The people groaned with relief and clapped, and one of the young women, with her blonde hair in a bun at the back of her neck, handed Walter her jug.

As if there were another, undamaged earth beneath all the rubble and dust, the wide stream revealed a mosaic star on the ground — a compass rose — and after Walter had both taken a drink and doused his face, the young woman asked quietly, 'What does tinned pineapple taste like?' She scratched the side of her nose with her little finger. 'Sweet?'

An ivory edelweiss hung from the breast of her dirndl and as he gave her back the vessel their hands touched fleetingly. 'Yes,' he said, aware that he was turning red. 'A little sweeter every day. We ate grass as well or it would have been unbearable.'

She laughed because she thought this was a joke, and he nodded to her and set off for the station. On either side of the street were ruins

180

several storeys high, and on some of the inside walls paintings or clocks still hung, a towel beside a shard of mirror. In front of a pile of stones, tracks had been laid for the trucks that were carrying the rubble away, which narrowed the street. If an army truck honked its horn, people had to step right into the rubble to get out of the way, holding on to twisted gas or water pipes and craning their necks to see what was on the flatbeds passing by. Many waved or tapped their lips with two fingers — a mute request for cigarettes — but the GIs seldom returned the greeting, and then only to children. To some they threw gumdrops or oranges.

The station was closed to civilians. In the shimmering air over the tracks the pylons and radio masts seemed to be moving or dissolving from one moment to the next. There was no glass in the curved arches of the crowded hall, the roof held up here and there by the trunks of spruce trees; hardly a wall wasn't cracked. The bars of the windows, melted into strange shapes in the intense heat of the nighttime raids, hung like steel foliage from the parapets, but in spite of the countless shell holes, the letters above the ticket counters could still be deciphered: 'Munich, Capital of the Movement!'

Nuns handed out tea and dried apple rings to the discharged soldiers, hundreds of them, from different services. They squatted or lay among rubble and broken glass on the platforms and looked mutely in the direction from which their train was supposed to come. Twisted tracks loomed into the sky, sleepers dangled from them. The walls of burned-out wagons that had tipped from the tracks were inscribed with chalk; addresses, missing person announcements, messages for those who had not yet been found. Beneath the crossed-out words 'Home to the Reich', someone had written 'Home to Mummy!'

★ ★ ★

Endless fields of rubble in Essen, too; the city centre looked as if it had been bombed even after not a stone was left standing. Alone and apparently undamaged, the huge synagogue on Steeler Strasse loomed into the summer sky, and had it not been for the traces of soot and smoke above its windows, older than the war, one might have been tempted to think of something like mercy, a protecting power.

The tram to Borbeck was full to bursting. People stood crammed together in dented cars with no windows, and Walter's journey took nearly two hours: time and again they had to get out and struggle on foot through craters full of twisted metal, broken pipes and sewage, to board another tram on the other side. The Persil advertisements on the green carriages were scratched, or had been blistered by the firestorms, and their wooden seats had been pulled out. The silent passengers were plainly starving, and even the gaunt faces of the conductors were darkened by grief. But the sound of the bell, the long shrill ringing when they pulled the cord on the ceiling, was just as

182

silvery and bright as before.

Outside the Lito in Frohnhausen, which only showed English-language films, children were trying to free chewing gum from the cobbles. Walter travelled as far as the monastery and then towards Klopstockstrasse. Sheds cobbled together from corrugated iron and floorboards stood behind the piles of rubble, and the smoke of wood fires filled the air. Some ruins had chicken wire stretched across them and were being used as stables; rabbits and chickens sat on cupboards, chests of drawers and white-spattered chairs, and in one bathroom a thin cow stood, eating hay from the tub.

In the rubble of the house where Walter had spent his childhood, the occasional blue tile gleamed in the exposed corridor. He climbed onto the mountain of bricks and looked round. All three aisles of St Dionysius — apart from a few pointed arches — had been destroyed, but the tower was still standing. The high chimney of the Linde bakery was only just held in shape by its steel rings. A crowd waited outside its newly barred door, which bore the inscription 'Essenausgabe/Food Distribution'; pots and milk churns clanged when bored children knocked them together. Then sparrows flew up from the bushes.

'Uschi, come and sit with Grandma!' called an elderly woman, and the girl who had been staring at Walter turned round. The cemetery wall had been hit as well, but the gatehouse where the undertakers worked on the ground floor looked unchanged. Not a single crack in the plaster or the black glass nameplate, not a slab of slate missing from the roof with the dormer window, Walter saw, as he turned the rusty handle, knocked the dust from his jacket and immediately stepped back in alarm.

As if she had been standing behind it, waiting, his sister opened the door without warning and said quietly, almost whispering into the vacuum, the sudden suspension of time: 'I knew, I dreamed it!' She smiled radiantly. 'My feather protected you!'

For a ghostly moment he saw their father's face, and she jumped from the step into his arms. The shadows in the corners of her eyes seemed darker, her shoulders bonier, and he spun her so violently through the air that her plaits flew and her velvet slippers fell on the stone floor. As soon as they had got their breath back he wrinkled his nose and asked, 'What's that smell? Have you taken up smoking or something?'

She wore a floral smock dress over tracksuit bottoms, and she pointed to the windows above the company sign, HESS UNDERTAKERS. 'Not me,' she said. 'It's Mum's boyfriend's birthday, he's turning a hundred and eighty or something. But he's plastered already, so you don't need to wish him many happy returns. He's snoring in his armchair and the others are drinking his Bols and smoking all his fags.' She reached between her lips and pulled out a long strand of gum. 'Do you want to try this? It's only a week old and still quite soft. At night I put it in an egg cup full of sugar, it sucks it all in and tastes sweet again.'

184

He pulled a face and they sat down on the front stairs. 'School's still shut, though we may be able to go back in August,' she chattered on. 'The whole roof is wrecked, can you imagine? In the meantime I'm teaching myself some things, particularly English. First of all we had the Yanks, with their brilliant swing music, and now we've got the Tommies. They're not so great because they're a bit boring, they hardly listen to any music and talk through their noses like teapots. But of course their chocolate tastes *spectacular!*'

A little boy riding a rusty bike along the pavement braked abruptly and swerved around her embroidered slippers. 'Good idea!' she called after him and winked at her brother. 'And soon I'm going to the north. There's a sanatorium in Glücksburg. The cough has got better, but Dr Böhmer says they're soon going to be opening even more mines than they had before the war. We're the engine of the economy, in fact, so the air's going to be so bad that you won't be able to hang your washing out ever again.' She stretched her big toes through the holes in her socks, then pulled them back in again. 'During the war, though, you have to admit, we had excellent air! I mean, when things weren't on fire. I could always breathe properly, even at night, and I stopped sweating all the time. I felt really healthy.' She pulled out some of the grass beside the stoop and let it trickle over Walter's fingers. 'And what about you? Have you got a girlfriend up there? I bet you have! Is she nice?'

He grinned, nodded, and without going any

deeper into the issue she lowered her head and tried to blow a bubble with her gum, but it was too tough and all she managed was a hard pop. She was holding her plaits together under her chin, and suddenly her eyes became moist and her lips went tight. 'What happened to Dad is terrible, isn't it? I wouldn't have thought I could miss him. Did Mum actually send you the telegram? I can't remember, I was in such a state. The same day my friend was dug out of the basement, Micky Berg, remember? The one you gave your Trix building set to? He was great, I went to school with him every morning. I always had to hold his glasses when he fought for me. And then they shovelled him out, and he sat there on a bench, covered in chalk and without his glasses. He looked like an old man.'

She sniffed, swallowed, spat her gum into the grass, and he put an arm around her shoulders and pulled her to him. Tears dripped onto his jacket and rolled over the waterproof fabric, and for a while neither of them said anything, just looked across the pile of bricks at the hospital. Fine hairs stood out on Leni's head and on her plaits, tickling Walter's neck, and it was so quiet in the street that he could hear her breath, the quiet whistling under her collarbone.

'Stay here,' she said at last and sniffed hard. 'They're looking for workers all over the place. You make good money as a miner and you get extra food, even butter and fresh milk — not that powdered muck. The miners' association gives you a flat, and we can move in together. I'll clean, wash the clothes and make your sandwiches. I'm strong, believe me, and it would get me away from that fat bastard at last. I mean, Dad was bad enough, but this guy . . . '

'How come?' Walter asked, leaning back and looking at her. 'What does he do? Does he hit you? Or does he get grabby?'

Leni grunted. 'I'd like to see him try! I'd stick the apple peeler in his ball sack. No, he's just disgusting, you know? He eats like a pig, the grease drips from his chin, and when you go into the bathroom he's standing there with his trousers at half-mast looking at his poo. And he has a box of watches and rings he collected from his dead people, can you believe it? Why should we bury those? he always says, the maggots don't wear jewellery. Good God almighty . . . ' She looked up at Walter, interlinked her fingers with his and asked quietly, almost timidly, 'How long are you staying?'

Walter shrugged. 'Depends on the trains. I've got my work up there, Leni, they won't keep the job open for me for ever. But if you come on your spa cure, we can see each other for longer, I promise. Glücksburg isn't at the end of the world. I'll collect you on the tractor and show you the farm and the animals and everything. We might even get the confiscated horses back, too.'

She grimaced as if the sun were shining in her eyes. 'Christ, don't talk to me like I'm a kid! I'm nearly thirteen! And I've been in love, I cried till my pillow was full. There was a captain here, David Reeve, a real film star. *Young lady*, he used to say, *take care, young lady*. He even had strawberry-flavoured chewing gum and his fingernails were always clean. But I've got over him now. The world doesn't owe you anything, you know, certainly not romance. Maybe I'll kiss a man once, just once, just to see what it's like, and after school I'll join the nuns over there.' She nudged him with her elbow, slipped into her shoes and smiled broadly. 'I don't suppose you want to kiss me, do you? Come on, let's go upstairs. It'll soon be feeding time.'

On the ground floor of the narrow house, coffin lids of various colours leaned against the walls with price tags hanging from their crosses. Behind the office with the Adler typewriter a flight of stairs behind a frosted glass door led to the first floor. The leaves of the rubber plant in the corridor gleamed, looking as polished as the linoleum, but the living room, where about twenty people were sitting and chatting in low voices, was grimy and full of smoke. The curtains were yellow, and Walter's sister pointed to a bald man in the armchair beside the window. He seemed to be asleep — with his chin on his chest, below which swelled a high belly, and both hands in his lap. His breath stirred the tip of the handkerchief in his jacket pocket, and one thumb twitched. 'That's him,' Leni whispered, and a few guests turned round. 'Mum's cash cow.'

The men were smoking cigars, as were some of the women, and they were all drinking wine with bits of fruit in it. Walter didn't know anybody apart from Herr Moritz, the old tailor from Kraftstrasse; they shook hands with him and leaned forward to understand his cheerful

188

greeting, which he whispered because he was suffering from a sore throat. A thin old man tested the fabric of Walter's uniform jacket between his fingers; Walter was about to explain where it came from when his mother entered the room.

Plumper than she had been before the war, she had put on lipstick and done her dark hair in waves, and at first she seemed not to see him. She blinked into the smoke. She wore a sleeveless red dress with a pearl brooch and a white apron. She said, 'Clear the middle of the table for me!' She was holding a big serving dish with crunchy bits of roast chicken and schnitzels in breadcrumbs on it, and while the guests moved their cups, glasses and ashtrays aside and unfolded their napkins, Leni linked arms with her homecoming brother and said, 'Look, Frau Urban, look who I've brought!'

But their mother set the dish down before she looked up, and Walter, who was having difficulty swallowing, knew that she had noticed him a long time before. Even though she was just forty-five, he noticed the skin on her neck hung wearily down; now she pretended to give a start and opened her mouth wide. Her eyebrows, raised high in surprise, made her forehead look even lower, and the theatrical clapping of her hands, with all their gold jewellery, embarrassed him, since he felt that it was all a performance for the benefit of her guests. Dark fluff grew around the corners of her lips, and her brown eyes were as cold as ever; Walter couldn't see himself in them.

'Cat got your tongue? Where did you pop up from?' she said at last, making way for a woman who was carrying bowls full of salad out of the kitchen. 'Couldn't you have let us know you were coming?'

The skin on her upper arms was already turning slack and uneven. She moved a potted plant so she could sit on a stool and look her son up and down, from his hair to his boots. For a moment she seemed to like what she saw; she had always found costumes, liveries and uniforms 'smart' or 'dashing', and she chuckled with amusement, biting the inside of her lip. But then she pressed her fists against her hips and shook her head as she looked around, seeing that there wasn't a chair free: 'My, my, my, where on earth are we going to put you? One more mouth to feed . . . '

Someone laughed, causing the sleeping man to give a start and open his swollen eyelids, and Walter, who had been about to walk over to his mother, lowered his arms again. Her gaze was unsteady, avoiding his. Sweat glistened in the wrinkles on her forehead as Walter snorted, smiled, clapped Leni gently on the shoulder and turned to leave. The front door was still open, and the ringing of a tram pulling a trailer full of rubble echoed in the stairwell, the wheels screeching as it took the bend.

Out on the pavement, children were playing with gun cartridges and shrapnel that they had arranged like table settings, and Walter's sister opened the window, bent over the still and called after him. But he couldn't make it out. He

190

jumped onto the platform of the tram and waved.

★ ★ ★

The wheat was almost ripe, the sky blue, the swallows flying very high. An amazing number of cows grazed in the meadows along the Eider, not just black-patched Holsteins but short-horned Nordic Reds as well. The air above the flowers flickered with the wings of insects, new beehives stood beneath the spruce trees in the park, and the weathercock that had once squeaked on the tower of the farmhouse had been replaced by a British flag.

The bus stopped in front of the stables, whose roof was being replaced. The sound of the wooden leggets with which the men were knocking the reeds into shape rang out between the walls, chaff stirred with each footstep they took. The former feed kitchen, with its mildewed walls, had been torn down, and Walter peered through the open door of the smithy. In the forge, beneath a white layer of ash, a handful of coals glowed, and a cut cervelat sausage hung in the chimney hood, but there wasn't a soul to be seen.

There was scaffolding in front of the farmhouse. The curved pillars of the portico and the coat of arms with the stallion under the sickles had been restored, the blown-out windows re-glazed and the slatted shutters painted green. Hollyhocks, roses and delphiniums blossomed by the doorstep. Walter lifted the

191

heavy knocker and let it fall against the door. Even though he could hear a typewriter clattering somewhere on the first floor, no one responded.

He walked through the shade of the lime tree in the courtyard and stepped into the byre. Several men, probably plumbers, were screwing nickel-coated pipes to the walls and under the ceiling. The big room was empty but there was an animal in the bull's box, a Belgian Blue with pale eyelashes; with its long, broad back and muscular hips, it must have weighed at least twice as much as ordinary bulls. Bran stuck to its muzzle and it snorted gently when Walter stroked the tuft of hair on its forehead as he asked the workmen about Thamling. Young swallows chirped in the hayloft.

No one knew where the manager was. Walter climbed the new outside steps, which had socks and shirts drying on the railings in the sun, to the milkers' rooms. It was almost dark in the corridor and he flicked the switch beside the door to no avail; there was no lightbulb in the rusty socket. But then someone started soldering down below — bright blue light flashed through the cracks between the floorboards and Walter could see into the bedrooms, which were now being used as archives and storage. Beside his bed, trunks and cardboard boxes, bedside tables with no drawers, old ewers and a bicycle frame were stacked up to the sloping wall.

The flame from the soldering iron crackled, the cobwebs gave off a silvery shimmer, and for a moment Walter paused outside the den where

Fiete had lived, looking at the pictures on the wall. They were clippings from newspapers and magazines: a half-naked dancer, the silhouette of a poet or philosopher with a pigtail, Hamburg harbour at night. Still hanging under the ceiling was the little basket in which Fiete had always hoarded a few apples, safe from the mice; Walter stepped over the threshold.

Old sea-grass mattresses were stacked high in the room and the cupboard in the wall wouldn't open more than a couple of inches. A smell of camphor and rancid milking grease struck Walter as he reached into the darkness, and he involuntarily closed his eyes. Tinware rattled, a book opened, and Walter felt his friend's work jumper under his fingertips — the one with the holes in it and the shoulder deformed by a hanger. He pulled it out.

Frau Isbahner's cat crossed the courtyard, a blue jay flew out of the lime tree. From between the stables, their thick brick walls, there came the sound of an engine, and the freshly planed railing of the outside steps vibrated quietly when Thamling came round the corner on a green painted tractor bearing the words 'John Deere'. The hay tedder behind it, set at an angle, was about five metres long, the tips of its circular spider's-leg forks gleaming in the sun. The old man held his hand over his eyes and called, 'Isn't that our Ata? Goodness, so you came back safe and sound?'

The air above the bonnet and around the vertical exhaust pipes shimmered; Thamling put the key in the breast pocket of his overall, climbed over the trailer coupling and held out his hand. The airstream had made his eyes run and his white moustache was yellow with nicotine. 'A bit thinner, but no matter . . . We'll fatten you up again.' He looked at the pullover in the crook of Walter's arm. 'That's a dreadful shame about the boy, isn't it? He always had a bee in his bonnet. And what's the point of being intelligent if you're not wise? Come on, I'm starving, let's grab a bite to eat.'

They walked past the open pigsty, where once again all the boxes seemed to be inhabited. Thamling shut the door in the gable side of the farmhouse and they washed their hands over the sink. Everything in the kitchen looked unchanged, and it was pleasantly cool as it always was in summer. Thamling filled a jug with tap water, set a bottle of Kümmel and two glasses on the table, and fetched a loaf of bread, a piece of ham and a smoked eel from the dining room. After Walter had fetched plates and cutlery from the dresser they sat down and began to eat.

The tall trees let only a little sun into the room, where a spiral of fly paper hung from the ceiling. Not all of them were dead — here and there a leg moved, or a wing, and sometimes a desperate buzzing could be heard. Then it would become silent again, apart from the ticking of the grandfather clock, and the old man smiled mildly when he noticed that Walter kept smelling the food, even the butter, and that he was dabbing up the crumbs with his thumb. Thamling cut up a few of last year's yellow apples and distributed the pieces on their plates.

194

He too looked thinner, his eyes lay in shadowy hollows, but his hands were as big as ever. The schnapps glass looked tiny between his fingers, and he drank it down, grunted gently and filled it up again. As he did so he looked into the park, where shorn sheep were grazing and two English officers sat at the stone table under the yew tree. Their caps and their ivory-handled sticks lay beside them on the bench. 'Hard work beats war, doesn't it? Whatever you've experienced, it'll stand you for the rest of your life, you'll see. How old are you now, twenty?'

Walter, whose mouth was full, shook his head, chewing and swallowing, and the old man took out a crushed pack of cigarettes. 'Just eighteen? The hell with them all!' The brass pendulum in the corner paused then, and a sudden whirring of cogs — the so-called breath of the clock — was followed by the striking of the hour, twice. 'Well,' Thamling added, lighting a Chesterfield, 'I guess he's already taken most of them . . . '

The clock ticked on, a lorry drove into the courtyard and stopped by the pigsty. Four soldiers jumped from the cab and the same number from the jeep with long aerials fastened to its windscreen that then pulled in behind. The men put on gloves and leaned a few planks with nailed-on battens against the back of the flatbed before they disappeared into the old building with the cross-shaped air holes in the wall. Jazz music came from the radio, trumpet notes, and a few moments later they drove a small herd of dappled pigs, their front feet bound, through the doorway. While a few soldiers beat them with pitchforks and cudgels, others pulled them by the ears up the ramp, which was far too steep, and when one of the animals slipped off the dung-smeared wood and dragged one of the soldiers down with it among the heavy bodies, Thamling turned away.

The laughter of the other men was louder than the squealing of the animals, and the old man blew out the smoke and said, 'I know what I promised you, Walter, and I would love to take you on again straight away. No one was as reliable as you. But I don't make the decisions here any more. Almost everything we produce is for the Allies now, as you see, and they're putting in machines for everything. When you've got the three hundred and fifty cows that we'll have next spring, it does make sense. You'd need countless specialists on staff, and we'd be paying out ridiculous sums in wages . . . It's best to do some serious investing.'

The officers outside flicked through some files, and Walter took a sip of water and said, 'Three hundred and fifty cows? And all the calves every year? Where are they going to graze here, Herr Thamling? They eat the grass quicker than it can grow.'

The old man nodded sadly. 'That worried me too, of course. But it's all going to work differently in future. The cows will just be penned in the byre all year, and they'll eat silage imported from South Africa. Calving will be done with block and tackle or by Caesarean section, and any idiot could work those modern

196

milking machines. They have these sophisticated vacuum pumps, you see, Walter . . . Not even a prize milker is a match for them. We're already doing it here, out on the outlying estate.'

Walter tipped back his schnapps, winced and stared straight ahead for a while. Only now did he notice the changes in the kitchen. Beside the radio was a black telephone with a lock in the dial. A fly ran across the table, over the rim of Walter's plate, and disappeared into the eel's pointed head; he held his fingers over his glass when Thamling tried to top him up. 'Well, great,' he said in a muted voice, 'then I've spent three years learning here for nothing, is that right? All that training for nothing.' He scratched his chin. 'I'd be best off going back to the Ruhr. They're looking for hewers and steelworkers and they don't pay too badly. A lot of pits have been reopened.'

Thamling nodded, opened the table drawer and took out a piece of paper. 'No war without milk, they always used to say, remember? Soon they'll be saying no milk without war. Every farm will go for the throats of every other, and in the end there won't be any farms left — only factories. But that'll take a while, son — the smaller operations can't afford the machines and cooling systems yet. For now, they're still milking by hand . . . and it's so much kinder that way. Every week, now, we have to amputate teats. That never happened before.'

He emptied his glass and passed the piece of paper across the table to Walter. 'Speaking of which . . . here, take a look at this. It's not the job I promised, but still good,' he went on. 'Pauly is an old friend, we were together in the first war, in the field hospital. Great chap, fouled things up nicely for the Food Production Estate. In fact, he breeds trotting horses, real champions, but he also has thirty-five dairy cows and he's urgently looking for a milking couple. Asked me if I knew anyone, and I told him about you. 'If he comes home safe and sound, he'd be perfect,' I said. 'He's conscientious, and so clean they call him Ata, like in the soap advertisement . . . ' And so on — I really talked you up. Go and see him straight away, before more refugees or returning soldiers show up and he can afford to pay you even less than he's offering now! You can take my car.'

Walter went to the window, where there was a bit more light, to read: 'Fahrenstedt farm near Böklund, 7 Spielkoppel, Telephone number 230', it said on the piece of paper, and Walter rubbed the back of his neck and said, 'A milking couple? But I don't have a wife, you know that.'

The old man got to his feet, screwed shut the schnapps bottle and cleared the dishes into the sink. 'Then marry one!' he replied. 'There are enough women fluttering about. Most of them have a dead husband in their luggage. They're just waiting for somebody new to scoop them up.'

He cut a big slice off the loaf of bread and wrapped it, along with the last of the ham, in a clean cloth, leaving them on the table for Walter. 'That little one you had in the winter, what was her name, Lisbeth, Lisa or something, she was

198

good, she milked here with the other women. Cheeky as a monkey and always had a cigarette in her mouth, but faster and more thorough than an apprentice. You should grab her while you can. She's working as a waitress in Kiel, in one of those navy dives.'

Thamling nodded and opened the door. 'Come on, then, son, I've got to get back to the hay while it's still warm. Take some of those apples, too. The car is in the stable.'

★ ★ ★

The unpaved road between the fields had been churned up by tanks, and when he looked in the mirror, Walter saw nothing but dust behind the VW's split rear window. An olive-drab four-wheel-drive Beetle with thick-grooved tyres, the car's engine clattered like a tractor's as Walter drove slowly along the Eider. The dark water flowed sluggishly, reflecting the sky and some scattered clouds, and a stork in the grass on the bank arched its neck and clattered the halves of its red beak together.

Walter drove up the hill and through the beech forest, which was less dense there. The remains of broken trees loomed, white and brown, from the shadows. Some trunks were charred, others were in splinters, but ferns were already growing again in the bomb craters. There were workers in blue Wehrmacht twill sitting on the drawbar of a rack wagon, eating their lunch and looking pointedly past Walter. One of them threw a handful of herbs into a pot that was steaming

199

away on a fire. In the grass lay the bloody pelt of a hare.

The light in the lofty avenue made Walter's hands look pale on the steering wheel; he stopped the Beetle by the edge of the forest and turned off its engine. Between mown meadows in which the hay had already been raked into long bales, the road twisted its way down to the ferry pier. Two women with bicycles were waiting there, watching carpenters working on the half-timbering of a bombed house. The new wood was reddish, amber tears sparkled here and there in the sun; a topping-out wreath of fir twigs was hanging on the roof ridge, streaming with brightly coloured ribbons.

The women wore headscarves knotted at the forehead, and as they chattered and laughed together, clearly about the young workmen, stripped to the waist, the ferry approached from the opposite bank of the canal. Part of the guardrail was missing, the windows of the wheelhouse were broken, and the white walls of the cabin were riddled with bullet holes already rusting at the edges. The engine must have been new, however — it was barely audible — and the bell was different too, smaller, gleaming as if it had been freshly polished. The blue municipal flag, with its silver anemone petals, was once again flying from the mast.

Water rushed up the cobbled approach, the gangplank was lowered, and Ortrud stepped from the wheelhouse and said something to her father, who was turning the winch. Her flaxen hair tied up at the back of her neck, she wore patched work trousers and an outsized man's jacket with the sleeves rolled up. After she had thrown a loop of rope over the bitt and a motorcyclist had driven ashore, she waved the waiting women on board.

Her father, almost unrecognizable under the frayed brim of his straw hat, was stuffing a pipe as Walter restarted the VW, keeping his foot on the clutch. Her face distorted, Ortrud grabbed at the small of her back with both hands and pressed her pelvis forward like someone in pain. Wind whipped over the hay and blew into her open jacket, and when she shaded her eyes with her fingers and tugged on the bell pull again, Walter shifted back into gear. He bit a hangnail from his thumb and waited under the beech trees until the gangplank had been winched up and green water foamed over the ferry's propeller shaft.

The motorcyclist rolled past him, raised a hand, but Walter didn't recognize the driver behind his goggles. The air tasted salty and the ribbons fluttered on the topping-out wreath. The pregnant girl in the ship's cabin drank something from a thermos as she took the wheel; her father lit his pipe, and the ship drifted almost silently, moving on a slant, towards the other side of the canal, where no one was waiting. Only a mailbag was left behind, lying against the bitt, and Walter closed his eyes for a moment and took a deep breath. Then he turned and drove off, between the paddocks and meadows full of carefully raked bales, towards Sehestedt, where there was another ferry pier.

★ ★ ★

Only a few buildings on Maklerstrasse still had their roofs intact, the walls topped with old tank tarpaulins or corrugated iron plates. The swastika over the door of the naval mess had been chiselled away from the relief, but its negative could be seen in the light from the setting sun. Walter parked Thamling's car beside a three-wheel truck full of barrels with English words printed on them. From the open windows of the inn came the smell of fried potatoes with onions and bacon. The men's laughter had the sound of schnapps.

Almost inaudible in the noise, a one-legged man in a wheelchair was playing the accordion. Walter threw a few coins into his hat and wound his way between the tables and chairs to the long bar, on which there stood a clock mounted on spiral columns. Bowls full of gherkins, pickled eggs and Kiel sprats stood on the buffet table, and the amber-coloured layer of aspic on the fish quivered when the waitresses walked by carrying heavy trays. One of them smiled at Walter, but most of the customers — dockworkers in oily canvas overalls and women in apron dresses — only looked at him and his American uniform out of the corners of their eyes, resentfully, Walter thought. No one stepped aside for him.

He was a little early. He pushed a basket full of umbrellas aside with the tip of his boot and ordered a beer from the woman by the tap, a thin old woman with her hair in curlers. At the other end of the counter, next to a telephone with scraps of a poster saying 'The enemy is listening!' still stuck to the wall above it, Elisabeth was drying cutlery. She exchanged a quick glance with Walter but didn't interrupt her conversation with a customer whose suit looked new, very smart, made to measure. She too was wearing new clothes, a dress and high heels, but her seamed stockings were already laddered.

'It isn't the end of the world . . . ' The accordionist struck up the first slow bars of the popular song, and the man talking to Elisabeth drained his brandy glass in one go. With pomaded strands of hair falling into his face, he twisted a ring from his finger and dropped it in the empty glass; Elisabeth tapped her temple and reached over the counter to straighten his tie, a sweat-drenched knot. As she did so she said something to him that sounded like an admonition, and at last the man nodded sadly, stroked her cheek and tottered outside.

She put the ring in her pocket, took Walter's beer from the landlady and approached him. As she did so, however, she kept an eye on the smartly dressed man's departure, as if she were concerned about him, and sure enough, just before he reached the door, he tripped over the accordionist's hat, and Elisabeth gave a half-smile. Her black hair was longer than before, and she had shaved her eyebrows and drawn in much more dramatic lines in their place. She was wearing lipstick, too, and it was only when she was standing right in front of Walter that she looked him in the eyes. 'Nice uniform.' She set his glass down. 'So where have you been all this time?'

Her charcoal dress had a wide collar, and there were pearls, framed in gold, in her earlobes. 'Me? Why?' Walter sipped from the foam. 'On a spa cure, of course. Didn't you get my letters?'

'What letters?' she asked, lighting a cigarette and studying the bottles on the shelves as if checking stock. She pulled a shred of tobacco from the tip of her tongue as Walter carefully ran his finger along the rim of his glass.

'Well, I didn't get yours either,' he said. 'They probably fell into enemy hands. All those passionate declarations of love . . . The enemy's going to be bursting with envy. I'm sure you wrote me lots, didn't you?'

At first she didn't reply. Resting her right elbow on the palm of her left hand, with her cigarette at eye level, she looked into the room. Her high heels had altered her posture: she looked prouder, with a confidently protruding bottom, and her breasts seemed bigger as well, which might have had something to do with the very pointed bra she was wearing. In spite of the smoke, Walter could smell her perfume, Old Lavender, and her blue eyes sparkled sternly when she asked, 'So what's all this, weren't you supposed to bring me something nice? Something embroidered?'

He frowned and drank again. 'Could be,' he said and wiped his mouth with the back of his hand. 'But you were supposed to tell me your size, weren't you?'

Chuckling, she tapped the ash off her

cigarette. 'Oh, Christ, I don't believe it! These farmers . . . The man goes to war and doesn't even bring me a back a blouse. But OK, it wouldn't have fitted anyway. Those women on the Puszta are a special breed, aren't they? Plump and fiery, from all that spicy food. Did you take them to the pictures? Or dancing?'

Walter shrugged. 'I only saw nurses. And prisoners in the camps.'

A bald man with a white fringe of hair pricked up his ears and leaned over the corner of the counter. He had big, bulging, bloodshot eyes. 'It was wrong!' he growled and drew on the cardboard cigar-holder. 'All that stuff about the Jews was wrong and stupid, kids, I've always said as much. Hitler shouldn't have locked them up in camps. And he certainly shouldn't have killed them.' He stuck out his damp lower lip, blew smoke into the air above him and waved his index finger like a pendulum. 'If they'd put a Jewish family in every attic, in every factory, on every bridge, or if they'd done the same with all those politicians, or the spies, I swear to you, not a single bomb would have fallen on our cities!'

Elisabeth, who was brushing her cigarette along the edge of an ashtray, raised her head. The fine wrinkles on her nose seemed to form a little rectangle, and her voice sounded unusually curt when she said, 'That's enough, Willi! Politics stay outside — when will you finally get that into your head? Any more of this and you'll have me to deal with. You'll be right out that door, you hear?'

She stared at the bald man, who finally

flinched. 'Yes, General! I beg your forgiveness.' He held his fingertips to his temples. 'Any chance of the same again?'

After she had brought Willi a beer and a schnapps, she rejoined Walter. Wide sunbeams fell slanting into the smoky room and made the ceiling look higher. The faces of the people in the shadows could hardly be seen now, and the ones in the light looked like shadows. Cigarettes glowed here and there, and even though it was noisy, Walter thought he could hear the faint sound of Elisabeth winding her watch. For a long time neither of them knew what to say, but there was nothing disconcerting about the silence — quite the contrary. Walter touched the rim of his glass again. 'What's up with it?' she asked at last and stubbed out her cigarette. 'Broken?'

'No,' he murmured. 'I'm just surprised. It feels so thin, so fragile.'

She hung her apron in a cupboard and looked in the mirror on the inside of the door. 'Beer glasses are like that. They've always been delicate.' With her hair loosened, she smoothed her dress and smiled at Walter. Above the white collar, her teeth looked greyer than he remembered. 'Come on, I'll show you my room. It's just up here, with a window overlooking the lock on the canal and my own bathroom.' And as he finished his beer she gave a sign to the woman at the tap and added under her breath, 'There's only cold water, but at least it means you won't burn your feet . . . '

She lifted a panel of the counter and emerged

on the other side, and hand in hand they pushed their way through the crowd. They climbed a narrow flight of stairs with coir runners to an attic floor with navy bunting and dusty model ships hanging from the ceiling and with what must have been at least a dozen doors. A ginger cat came towards them — a thin creature with a quivering, upstretched tail — and darted away in alarm when Elisabeth hissed at it. 'This is my kingdom,' she said, taking a key from her pack of cigarettes.

It was a little garret, a small bedroom, with a mirrored wardrobe and a bed with a carved headboard. On a shelf on the wall there was a tin cup holding an immersion heater, and a bunch of roses wilting in a window niche. The parchment shade of her lamp was scribbled with numbers, phone numbers, perhaps, and no sooner had Elisabeth closed the door than Walter pulled her to him. He wrapped his arms around her waist, but she turned her face away and pushed him back. 'Hey, hey, hold your horses! You're scratchy . . . '

Groaning, she slung her shoes in the corner. Then she put her watch on the bedside table, unbuttoned the collar from her dress, and pulled two white cloths out from under her armpits. She wanted to look as delicate as a young girl as she stood before him in her stockings and entwined her fingers behind his neck to kiss him her way, very gently. After that, her lips were paler, with only a little red in the corners, but the blue of her eyes looked darker. She lay down on the bed and smoothed the empty space next to her. Seabirds cried above the roof.

'What did the man with the tie want from you?' Walter asked, hanging his jacket on the door handle, pulling his boots off, lying down next to her. The stains on her pillow smelled of hair-cream or pomade, fine quills poked through the pillowcase. 'Why did he give you his signet ring?'

A gurgling sound came from the bathroom, which had no door, just a yellow, waxed cloth curtain. Plates clattered in the kitchen below. She pulled a bit of fluff from his hair. 'Black Market Freddy? Oh Christ, he's a sad case,' she said. 'A soak. He always leaves that bauble here so that he has an excuse to come back to the pub the next day. He was just flirting with me.'

'Really?' Walter stared at the water stains on the ceiling and the holes in the plaster with straw hanging out of them. In one spot, the rusty joints of the tin roof were exposed. 'I'm sure he's quite a catch. You can tell he's loaded.'

She unbuttoned his shirt and touched his chest. 'Yes, he's rich, all right. And he looks after himself. Reeks like a pharmacy and rabbits on endlessly. He says I'm his dream girl, and always calls me 'Gypsy Queen'.'

'And why did you turn him down?'

'What makes you think I did? He's one of many admirers, my friend. All I did was tell him he's too short for me. That I need a tall man. Have you always had hairs on your chest?'

Walter lowered his chin and looked down at himself. 'No idea. Probably . . . I'm getting the feeling it's not a good idea to be too sensitive around you — have I got that right? That Freddy might have a growth spurt, one of these days, or I suppose he might have other, hidden charms . . . What about me, am I tall enough for you?'

Foghorns sounded in the distance, and Elisabeth blushed. Or perhaps it only looked that way: evening sunlight glowed in the full-length mirror on the wardrobe. 'Of course there are taller men . . . ' she said, and moved the flap over his fly to one side. 'Well, look, what have we here? A real zip fastener?' She ran the back of her painted fingernail along the brass teeth. 'They're always in a hurry in America, aren't they?'

He shrugged. 'I don't know, I've never been there. At least it means you don't lose as many buttons.'

His fingers trembled as he tucked some strands of hair behind her ear. Her hair was thin, and blunt from the curling tongs. 'Have you ever thought about our phone conversation, Liesel?'

She opened her mouth, apparently perplexed. 'What's there to think about it? All I heard was someone saying 'I'm back', and then a kind of stammering on the line . . . Was that a phone conversation?'

Walter sat up, the old bed creaked, and when Elisabeth raised her head and opened her little eyes, as anxious as before, he saw the shadows of her shaved eyebrows beneath her make-up. 'Listen,' he said hoarsely. 'I only had a few coins, there was this sign that said 'Keep it short!' and there were people waiting outside . . . I mean, if you really want, we could do it in church. Frau Thamling would lend us her wedding dress. She

209

showed it to me, you'd hardly notice the smell of mothballs. And I'm sure my mother would send us rings. We've known each other for a while, and it might just work out. Being part of a couple is easier, and nicer too in a lot of ways. You'd just have to come with me to the byre . . . '

He took her hand, and for a few heartbeats she didn't say anything. The curl fell over her ear again and she sighed deeply. 'God almighty, if that doesn't beat everything,' she said at last. 'Even that spiv. Who'd have guessed?' Although she seemed to be amused, her eyes looked disheartened. ''You'd just have to come with me to the byre'! . . . I don't think anyone's ever had such a romantic proposal!'

She pulled away from him, and he sank back against the headboard. The carvings pressed into his back, the wooden fruits and flowers. 'So?'

But Elisabeth, resting her chin on her hand, was busy with his zip again, pulling it up and down. 'So what?' she replied. 'Don't ask such stupid questions! Who gets married at seventeen if they don't have to? And anyway, I'm glad to be in a town at last. I like it here, I've got friends, clothes, pretty shoes. The boss's daughter never came back from Neuengamme, so I can wear her stuff. On Sunday I walk to the harbour, to the ocean liners, where the sailors in their white uniforms whistle at me — and you want to drag me back to the sticks?'

He nodded thoughtfully. 'The farm is in great shape, I can promise you that. Near Schleswig, I took a look at it yesterday. Thirty-five dairy cows and a bull, a prize-winning bull at that. His name's Mozart, like the singer. But they'll only take on a married milking couple, of course, to save on a farm hand.' He slipped down deeper and nestled against her. 'We can live rent-free in a little house on the edge of the field, you know. Three well-furnished rooms plus garden and wages in kind, which means one pig a year, geese, eggs, flour. No one to tell us what to do as long as we milk, keep the byre in order and bring the milk to the dairy in Böklund. There's a horse cart for the churns. And there's a dance with different bands every Saturday — then on Sunday I could look after the cows on my own, and you could sleep in. What do you say?'

She didn't reply, just clicked her tongue indignantly, and when Walter got his breath back she grabbed him by the ears and whispered into his mouth, 'Just shut your trap, will you?' Sharp fingernails, a painful grip, but her lips were softer and fuller. She pulled her dress over her head, undid her bra; he took off his trousers, still lying down, and then he felt the buttons of her suspenders on her thighs, the cool nylon seams, and her black curls tickled his cheek as she said, 'And now pay attention . . .'

Shadows darted through the room and turned into seagulls when they brushed the mirror. The bed wobbled, the head struck the cast-iron radiator, and Elisabeth, with the tip of her tongue between her teeth, didn't close her eyes as she moved, or only briefly, at the very last moment, when she also closed her mouth tight. And a little later they lay still, side by side, staring at the ceiling and waiting for their

211

heartbeats to subside, for the sweat on their skin to cool and the quiet sadness for which they had no words to fade. Darkness fell slowly.

★ ★ ★

They slept for about an hour and woke up when a beam of light flashed through the window from the canal. Elisabeth sat up, rolled off her stockings and opened her flesh-coloured garter belt. The hanger on which she had hung her dress had a crocheted cover. The miaowing of the cat came from the corridor, its scratching at the door, which only fell silent when she threw a shoe. She pulled a half-full bottle of wine from behind her roses and showed Walter the label, a fat monk. 'Doesn't he look like old Hunstein, the farmers' leader? What a bastard he was, incorrigible. His forced labourers finally lynched him. The rope broke twice, and in the end they had to use fencing wire.' She bit her lip to keep from smiling. The cork broke when she pulled it out; she removed the remainder with a pair of scissors, filled a tin cup and held it out. 'You first, you're the guest. I've already raised a glass. Let's drink to Fiete.'

The wine was almost black, and though it smelled good, it tasted strangely metallic. Elisabeth lay down beside him again, snuggled against his shoulder, stroking the hair on his chest. As she did so she looked dreamily out of the window, and Walter drank again, but his mouth felt drier with each sip. His teeth were on edge as well.

'Deserting . . . ' Elisabeth said softly and slowly, as if speaking a foreign language. 'Crazy, don't you think? Why would he do something like that when he knew how dangerous it was? He was usually so clever . . . Couldn't you have kept an eye on him?'

Walter frowned. 'Was I his big brother? He was fighting in a completely different unit.'

She studied him. Her scent of lavender had almost fled.

'I warned him, of course,' Walter went on. 'Everyone was afraid of Siberia, of forced labour camps . . . But the Hungarian-Germans couldn't be trusted to hide you . . . they only pretended to be on our side . . . they'd blow the whistle on deserters as soon as their backs were turned . . . and the military police were all over the place, searching every barn and bog. Fiete had no chance on the plains, which are so flat you can see in the morning what's going to happen in the afternoon . . . But he didn't listen to me — he just wanted to get back to his Ortrud.'

She gently stroked his cock. 'And what about you? Didn't you want to come back to me?'

Some wine dripped into the hollow of his throat as he handed her the cup. 'Of course I wanted to get away. But I wasn't on the front lines . . . I was just standing around while all that madness went on. I barely fired a shot . . . or only one, to be precise. So I was in less danger of dying in battle than of being executed if I tried to run away.'

Elisabeth sat up; her pearls shimmered dimly, the light from the lock on the canal shone in her

213

hair. Her cheeks pale, she stared sightlessly into the distance, and while she drank her eyes glistened. 'But who — ' she asked hoarsely — 'who could bring himself to do something like that? I mean, the men who shot him, weren't they comrades, boys like Friedrich? Didn't they have any qualms about killing him? They aimed and fired, just like that?'

Walter closed his eyes for a moment. 'Yes, what an idea. What have you got left? Either you carry out the order or you refuse to . . . and if you refuse, that's your own death sentence, which will also be ruthlessly enforced. That's you up against the wall. There's only one consolation, a faint one — in one of the rifles there's always a blank, at least if it's a comrade who's due for the chop. So everyone in the firing squad can imagine he wasn't responsible. A matter of morale . . . '

Elisabeth set the cup down beside her ashtray and waited for Walter to go on, but he was done. The floodlight on the lock went out. 'Were you there?' she asked in an undertone, almost whispering. 'Did you see it?'

His stubble rustled as he ran his fingers over his chin, and it might have been because of the sudden darkness that his human silence seemed somehow more audible than the room's own, natural stillness. The repeated mewing in the corridor didn't change any of it, and neither did the foghorn outside, so close and tuned so deeply that the thin panes shook. 'I saw a lot,' he said at last and swallowed. 'Too much, if you ask me. But that was the war.'

214

Elisabeth wiped her eyes. She'd put her thumb on the switch of her bedside lamp, though hadn't turned it on yet. It seemed that she must have been concentrating closely on Walter's answer, for a time, drawing her lower lip over her upper as she often did when she was thinking. Soon, however, she shook her head — a short, energetic movement, as if she were crossing something out inside herself — blew a curl away from her forehead, and said quietly, 'Poor boy. He deserved better.'

Walter drank again from the bitter wine. 'Of course,' he said. 'So did we all.'

Elisabeth took a deep breath. 'Oh, no, not you,' she said and turned the light on. There was a charred spot where the bulb touched the plissé shade. 'Absolutely not you, my boy. You've got the best thing of all — me!' Smiling, she ruffled his hair and reached into her bedside table, in which dozens of packs of cigarettes were stacked, handing him a bar of chocolate. When she went to the bathroom, he saw a glistening streak on her thigh. 'Don't throw the silver paper away,' she called from behind the curtain. 'I collect it.'

He didn't ask what for, and tore the packaging open. Too hungry to let the Cadbury's bar melt in his mouth, he chewed it greedily like bread. It tasted of rum and raisins, and while Elisabeth let the bathwater run so that he couldn't hear her peeing, he smelled the pillowcase again and couldn't help sneezing. He picked a few reddish cat hairs from his lips and looked around her room, at the wardrobe with the suitcase on top of it, the little table under the dormer, the shelf

215

on the wall. Apart from some ornaments and a candle, there were books on it. A few Brockhaus volumes, *Grand Hotel* by Vicki Baum, *Beneath the Wheel* by Hermann Hesse, an old Bible.

A bell rang in the taproom. Elisabeth washed herself, spluttering and shivering; Walter reached up and flicked through the worn leather volume. It had faded gilt edging and some of the corners were turned down. Dried autumn leaves and a few inflation banknotes from 1923 slipped out from between the pages, in denominations of several million, and when Walter ran his hand over a psalm he could feel the letters under his fingertips.

He had never read the Bible before. He struggled to decipher the gothic script, particularly since the words on the following or previous pages showed through the thin paper. Words like *hind* or *Leviathan* meant nothing to him, and often he only vaguely grasped what each sentence was trying to convey . . . but their cadence, all their repetitions, nonetheless exerted a sort of gravity upon him, and soon he felt as though the rhythm of his breathing was being altered, as though the verses were compelling his lips to move; he took a sip then and read a few lines from the first book of Moses at a conversational volume — and the faint echo this caused in the cup made it sound as if someone was speaking along with him.

Elisabeth stepped out from behind the waxed cloth. 'What's that you said?'

But he didn't reply, only scratched the spot with his thumbnail and set the Bible back on the

216

shelf, making the plank shake slightly. 'I inherited all those old books,' Elisabeth said proudly, pulling a nightdress over her head. She had removed her pearls, and the holes in her ears were red. 'A student used to live here. A poor poet. Apparently his bed never got cold. By the way: were you careful?'

'What about?' Walter asked, taking another bite of the chocolate as Elisabeth lit a cigarette. There was a stern wrinkle over her nose, but her thin mouth seemed to be smiling.

'Oh terrific! And what happens if I get pregnant?'

He shrugged. 'Then you'll put on weight. But only for nine months.'

'Oho! What a nerve on this guy!' She blew smoke at the lamp. 'He makes you fall in love with him and then he thinks . . . Maybe you want to have a son, is that it? A son and heir, an heirloom, or whatever the word is. And then we'll build a house, plant a tree — it sounds very exciting. Aren't you going to wash?'

'Don't care,' he said. 'Could be a daughter. I'd even prefer that.'

'No, no, you want a son, be honest. The milker's son . . . ' She lay back on the bed and stroked his arm. 'What would that make him? Some sort of milking champion?'

Walter reached for her cigarette, took a deep drag, and was surprised that it didn't make him cough. 'I don't care what he does,' he said, tasting the smoke. 'Time, or fate or whatever, will sort that one out. As far as I'm concerned he can be what he likes as long as he isn't a soldier.'

217

He took another drag and looked her over. Even though she was young, there were already fine wrinkles on her cheekbones. 'So, what about this farm, Liesel? Have you had a think? It doesn't have to be for ever. Eventually they'll switch to machines, and we'll go to the mines in the Ruhr — you can make good money there, too. And you'd be back in a city.' He cleared his throat. 'We just need to make our minds up — it's the first of the month at the weekend. Are you coming?'

There was no music from the bar now, no voices. The clatter of plates in the kitchen had stopped as well. Elisabeth turned out the light again with the faintest of clicks. It was completely dark for a moment, and she pressed herself against him; he rested a hand on her shoulder blade. The moon couldn't be seen through the window, but its light turned their smoke blue and quivered on the edges of the furniture and in the facets of the mirror like the reflection of a longing almost forgotten out of sheer exhaustion. And then she said quietly, 'Yes.'

Epilogue

Took the train as so often in early March, weary after a hard-working, apparently endless winter, grateful for the peace in the compartment, the coffee brought by the refreshments service, looking eagerly through the landscape for the first blossoms. But nowhere so much as a bud, a fresh blade; in the ploughed fields beyond Berlin only dry earth, empty pallets in the greenhouses, and in a hollow what looked like an encampment of greyish-brown deer turned out on closer inspection to be piles of stones and their shadows. The reeds by the quarry ponds are still fallow, the sun isn't strong enough to brighten the dark water, and there's frost to come. Near Magdeburg, ice on the tracks, thin snow, a cloudbank before reaching Braunschweig. And yet the profound desire for spring is already giving the bare birch trees on the horizon a tinge of green.

My parents' grave was to be levelled — unless I decided to extend the lease. It was tended by an aunt, my father's sister, who planted it with pansies, begonias or heather depending on the season, and put a light on it at All Souls'. A melancholy chain-smoker who always knew where the Jägermeister was, she was the last living relative from my parents' generation and refused to let illness or loneliness deprive her of her sense of humour. Once when I invited her to

219

Café Kloos, she wouldn't set her cigarette down save to chew or talk, saying, 'This crumb cake is good. I'd like to eat it at my funeral.'

The cemetery was on the edge of Oberhausen, and as I wanted to travel on to Belgium anyway, I'd decided to go via the Ruhr. You could count on one hand how many times in the last twenty-five years I'd put flowers on the gravestone, and I wasn't sure if I would bother to extend the lease on the plot. Apart from Aunt Leni, who had already indicated that planting and raking were getting to be too much for her, and who wanted to be buried next to her husband anyway, most of my parents' acquaintances were dead — so what was the point in keeping the grave?

And yet something in me resisted the idea of letting it be levelled — perhaps superstition, fear of misfortune or some sort of curse, I didn't know. I would make the decision at the cemetery. The initial lease had been signed by my father, I saw only now, in the old-fashioned Sütterlin script he had always used, already a little unsteady from the cancer. Below the family name, the date, and the number of the plot there was a red stamp: *Plot lease terminated*.

Just before I reached Bielefeld, it actually began to snow, a dense flurry, and the train stopped again and again. Dusk was breaking as I arrived in Oberhausen, and I left my suitcase in the Ruhrland Hotel and took a taxi, the only one outside the building. 'Where to?' asked the driver, with his grey ponytail, solving a Sudoku puzzle and listening to the radio — a Schubert

Lied. 'Follow the music,' I said, and he put his hands, covered with silver rings, on the steering wheel, looked over his shoulder and frowned, which looked a little threatening. Two tears were tattooed below his right eye. He grinned when I added, 'To the cemetery, Tackenberg.'

'*Fremd bin ich eingezogen,* / *Fremd zieh ich wieder aus*' — 'A stranger I came, a stranger I leave'. Big snowflakes fell against the panes but weren't sticking yet on the busy roads towards Sterkrade — only appearing as grey slush that sprayed up under the wheels of the cab or dripped from the billboards we passed. But as we drove towards the stadium things started to change: the car skidded through ruts that got deeper and deeper until the heavy, wet snow was crunching under the floor panel, and the driver was cursing quietly. We inched our way past the sports ground, past the Schätzlein supermarket, past my former school. No footprints in the white playground, not a soul to be seen, and the hawk sitting on the mosaic fountain was made of plastic; I assume it was there to scare the pigeons.

Light from the streetlamps shone through the windows into a corridor in the school building — you could see into the classrooms, where the shadows of snowflakes fell on chairs, tables and blank blackboards. The silent building always looked more disquieting empty, during a holiday or on a weekend, than it ever had during lesson times — perhaps because those rectangular, consecutively numbered buildings, their stark architecture, laid bare the true inhumanity of

221

their purpose without the camouflage of people present. But perhaps too because that place, empty, demonstrated better than any graveyard what the world would look like if we all ceased to exist one day, and all that remained of what was dear and important to us was the blurred chalk traces of words and numbers on a blackboard.

'I do not wish to trouble your dream / To lose your peace would be a shame / You should not hear my step . . . ' The driver turned into Elpenbachstrasse, an old avenue of plane trees that stood amid brick cottages with dead straight hedges and curtains like elegant lines of French in a German text. I asked him to stop in front of the graveyard's nursery and gave him a considerable tip not to drive away; getting a taxi around there was only possible at the cost of an endless wait. Then I stamped through the snow to the little flower shop beside the gate and bought one of the ready-made bouquets in the window: white tulips, conifer twigs and mimosas.

The cemetery had recently been enlarged. The Calvary had been removed and the gardens behind it cleared, and the little open-air swimming pool on the neighbouring property, which had been closed even when I was a child and had been used as a pasture by the previous tenant — 'Stop leaving me your old bread!' he'd once painted on his house. 'My horse has been dead for five years!' — was now a burial ground as well. All was white; they'd only cleared the path to the new chapel, and in the deep snow little could be seen of the graves beyond the

222

occasional back of a stone or the tip of an obelisk.

I strode off in the direction I remembered, past a single red candle flickering crookedly on a snowdrift, and after only three or four steps I was no longer on the path; something crunched and creaked under my feet as if I was walking on old wreaths. Last time I'd seen it, the grave had been next to a hedge, but there was no sign of the privet now as I walked around an enclosure filled with rubbish — black, red and gold ribbons, plastic roses and withered chrysanthemums hung from the lattice-work — and suddenly sank up to my knees, clinging to a boulder.

The entire landscape fell away towards the mine where my father had once worked, all that remained of which was the pithead, black with resting crows. Monuments and crosses ran to the edge of the forest, and between them were strange paths and bare trees, as if glazed by ice. With snow in my shoes I made several more attempts in one direction or another, stumbled over invisible stairs, tripped over hidden borders and wiped a few gravestones clear, tearing my glove on the reliefs, but couldn't find my parents' grave.

It was getting dark. A gurgling sound came from beneath the layer of ice that covered a pond and a hare leaped away; I gave up looking. I followed my own footsteps back to the ruby candlelight, sputtering now, and left my bouquet beside it, pausing there for a moment. Hardly any wind, and it had stopped snowing; a little way off, where the taxi's exhaust fumes were sweeping along the road, the lights of the flower shop still burned, and although the snowflakes had fallen without a sound, scattering in silence, it was now, somehow, more silent still.